STALINA

a novel

EMILY RUBIN

PUBLISHED BY

amazon encore

2/11

The characters and events portrayed in this book are fictitious.
Any similarity to real persons, living or dead, is coincidental
and not intended by the author.

Published by AmazonEncore
P.O. Box 400818
Las Vegas, NV 89140

ISBN-13: 9781935597179
ISBN-10: 1935597175

For Anne

Acknowledgments

Thanks to the students in my "Oral History" class at Touro College in Brighton Beach, Brooklyn for sharing their life stories, which inspired the writing of this novel.

Thanks to the Summer Literary Seminar for the opportunity to visit and write in Russia.

To my friends, too many to name here, who helped me get to Russia because they knew it was important.

To Terry Goodman of AmazonEncore whose phone call about publishing this book was like winning the lottery.

Special thanks to Linda Rosenberg for her insightful editing and for meeting me on train platforms to hand off her weekly notes.

To Les Baum for sharing everything with me and for those encouraging nudges to keep writing.

To Anne Kristy Childers, in memory of her warm laughter and exceptional intelligence.

*"Just as the future ripens in the past,
so the past smolders in the future."*
Anna Akhmatova

Prologue: Birthday

I was eighteen years old on the third of March, 1953. My mother allowed me to invite three friends to celebrate in our tiny Leningrad apartment.

"Why only three?" I complained.

"There are no parties permitted while Stalin is so ill. If three come, it's not officially a party, but you still must be very quiet."

My mother often turned the truth on its side to explain things she did not want to talk about. Stalin lay on his deathbed for days, and all of Soviet Russia listened to radio reports of his failing health around the clock. My mother feared any backlash if jocularity was heard from our apartment during so solemn a time.

"How many people make a party?" I asked and showed her the design I wanted to make for the top of my cake. I had drawn a big, broad apple tree filled with fruit.

"Four," she said, "not including the host, because then you have two couples who can play cards while the host serves tea. No more about that. What will you use to decorate your birthday cake?"

My mother's answer about four making a party was made up, just like the story about my father fighting the fascists.

By that time he was already dead, starved to death in a prison I never knew to visit.

"Sour cherry drops for the apples, spearmint gums for the leaves, and chocolate sticks for the branches and body," I explained.

My mother told me I was clever.

The "not-a-party" birthday was on a Monday after school. I carefully chose my guests—Amalia, who always wore a worn-out red velvet ribbon in her hair; Alma, who had one crossed eye; and Olga, whose mother let her cut her own hair. I served layer cake with icing made from plums and fruit compote. To keep the party a secret from our neighbors, we agreed to be like the silent film stars Mary Pickford, Charlie Chaplin, and Rudolph Valentino—responding to anything, happy or sad, with our faces and bodies, no sound allowed. It was great fun, and my mother could keep her uninterrupted vigil at the crackling radio without worrying about a visit from the black uniforms and leather boots of the police. Two days later Stalin died without waking. My mother, who named me after him, was never the same. That was a long time ago. Everything is very different now.

Chapter One: Reds

To begin my story, I offer this blunt self-portrait, the real Stalina Folskaya. My nose is long and pointy and slightly skewed to the right. My arms are thick and well muscled with just a bit of softness on the underside. Gravity of the flesh comes with age, as I have recently reached my sixty-seventh year. I still have a strong back and shapely, wide hips. Most pleasing to me are the long, slender fingers of my hands. I keep my nails carefully manicured and painted a deep red called "Heart Stopper" from Revlon. My grandmother Lana used to pick at the skin around her thumbnails, and I do the same. I have her hands exactly, even down to the ridges on my right thumbnail. Yet, it is hard to believe I am now, in 2002, almost the same age she was when she died. How can that be? In Russia, years before I came to the USA and the Liberty Motel, a palm reader once told me the indentations on the nail represent a deeply buried pain that has not yet surfaced, but will someday. I paid her only two rubles for the five-ruble reading because she could not tell me more about this "pain." I left the last three rubles clutched in my unread palm.

I said to her, "I have experienced much heartache because of stupid, selfish people. That is pain enough."

She yelled after me, "Don't be stingy with your future, Stalina. Pay the three rubles, and I'll tell you about the pain! You will be much better off."

"I like not knowing," I responded.

That was a very difficult time. It was 1991, and the Soviet Union was finished. My world was bankrupt. I had much to think about. It was then I started to color my hair. Brunette was my true color, but I find black more dramatic for my pale skin. In Russia I used a dye made in Cuba called "Zarzamora," which means blackberry bush. My friend Olga, who grew up to run her own hair salon, would get the hair dye along with boxes of Cohiba cigars from a comrade in Havana. She used the cigars for bribes on the black market when her salon was running low on hair spray and nail polish. Here I use L'Oreal's "Blackest Black," a less deep but longer-lasting color. From the back, my head looks like a bush filled with shiny black crows. The abundance of hair makes me appear larger than my five-foot frame. With my rugged Russian looks, I choose never to go into public without makeup. My dark brown eyes are always lined with black kohl and my eyelids a little covered with a creamy blue eye shadow called "Sky Blue" from Coty. I like to call the eye shadow "Leningrad Blue" because it reminds me of the sky above the Neva River back home, when the long days of summer sunlight make the blue sky pale, soft, and forgiving. My lipstick is a dark blood red called "Can-Can" from Revlon. I read in *Russian Woman* magazine that red lipstick gives lips a full, attractive, sexy appearance and communicates a well-developed ego.

I dress comfortably in black stretch leggings and blouses of washable silk. I wear a lab coat at work over my clothes. As an employee of the Liberty Motel, my old lab coat is very useful. There will be more about my workplace later, but now I will tell you about leaving my mother and my country.

Chapter Two: Good-bye

It was late September in 1991 when I said good-bye to my mother, Sophia, at her rooming house for the elderly on Lermontovsky Prospekt. At seventy-nine, she was too old and too stubborn to leave Leningrad.

"Fine, stay," I always replied.

My mother's room in the defunct school had high ceilings, a cement floor, and six metal-framed cots set against faded pink plaster walls. Smells of rusting metal and boiled cabbage filled the air and made it heavy, but nourishing to our complexions. The last time I was there, we were alone, but even so we spoke in whispers simply out of habit.

"I don't like your hair that color," she said.

"The black?" I replied as I positioned a photograph of my father above the headboard of her sagging cot. "Shall I hang the picture of Father here?"

"You look like a whore," she added.

I had taken that picture of Father outside our dacha near Lake Ladoga, north of Leningrad, shortly before he was arrested in 1952. He was gardening in the blue coveralls he wore for his job at the loading docks at the shipyards on the Neva. He took that job after the school where he taught literature fired him for assigning *The Scarlet Letter* to his students. The headmaster disapproved of Hawthorne's provincial attitude. My father thought it told things in a very human way and tried to defend his course of teaching. It could have been any book—they just wanted to get rid of him. It was a bad time to be a writer and a Jew. The job at the docks was grueling. He would come to the dacha on the weekends very tired, but would go to work in the garden as soon as he arrived. My mother would have a bush or tree she wanted planted, and she would promise to make his favorite mushroom blinis if he dug holes for a rhododendron or two. He was saddened about not teaching, and I once saw him late at night from my window burying his books in the holes. He thought it would protect them—this time from the censors. During wartime our city buried many monuments and works of art to protect them from the bombs.

Father read to me in English. It was his favorite language. A good balance for our harsh Russian minds, he would say. Every night until I was thirteen he filled my head with Shakespeare, Steinbeck, and Dickens. Big books, every word, one at a time. He laughed at the attitudes of French and Italian, and was uncomfortable with the wild tempo of Spanish. I am not partial, but from him I learned my English very well. Then he was gone.

But back to my mother. "I think it looks dramatic," I said, referring to my hair color as I hammered a nail into the wall with the heel of my shoe.

The photograph was the only decoration in the room. I sat on the cot next to my mother and stroked her arms up and down gently, tickling the hairs along her raised blue veins. She slowly rocked back and forth. Her crippled hands, which had once kneaded mounds of flour and water into sourdough bread, felt dry and brittle, like kindling that could be snapped.

"What's that smell? You ate garlic?" she said, sniffing in my direction.

She hated garlic, and I'd had garlic soup for lunch.

"Father looks handsome in that picture, don't you think?"

"Police eat garrr-lic…I itch."

"Where?" I asked.

"My ass has sores from the sandpaper they use for sheets."

"Petroleum jelly?" I had packed some with her things.

"You're a hussy who fucks the police!"

"Moth—" I stopped myself.

No point to protest.

She continued, "Don't touch me, you reeking whore!"

I had grown accustomed to Mother's ill-tempered dementia. The five other women who shared her room also ignored her rants. A bare light bulb dangling from the ceiling cast shadows of the six cots and divided the room into long, dark corridors. A burning coal stove left a darkened halo of soot on the pink plaster ceiling. I was sweating, and my mother had difficulty breathing. The roommates were at the commissary having tea and cake. Mother waited till they finished because she preferred not to talk to them and liked the tea at its darkest, from the bottom of the samovar.

"I need it strong for my digestion," she would say.

"Would you like me to walk you downstairs?" I asked.

"And then are you also going to wipe my ass?"

"No, Mother. Good-bye, Mother."

I kissed her forehead and left her sitting at the very edge of the cot, her stockinged feet barely touching the floor. The starch in her flowered dress helped her to sit up straight, and the dampened heat of the room made her white hair into a frizzy, glowing halo. She looked like a mad angel awaiting a task from the Almighty.

She yelled after me, "I'll be dead soon, Stalina. Remember, you ate cake while Stalin lay dying!"

Leaving her room, I looked through the hallway windows at the clouds hanging high above our newly renamed St. Petersburg. I imagined my angel mother soaring with wings spread wide, shouting her words down to earth like a trumpet: "Come near me and I'll show you my ravaged ass, then I'll take a nip of yours and spit it down your throat! I'm going to cripple you to your toes with nausea, that way you cannot leave me."

Walking down the hallway, I could hear her rugged smoker's cough followed by a wet gurgling sound from deep within her lungs.

I thought, "She's my mother and I know it's wrong, but I won't miss cleaning up her raving angel ooze."

It was a long, noisy walk down the marble corridor to the nurse's station. The nurse on duty grabbed my bribe of a box of twelve brassieres right out of my hand. They would sell or trade easily in post-Soviet Leningrad, and I wanted my mother to have special attention. I was given three boxes of brassieres and a carton of toilet tissue as salary from my last month of work at the laboratory where I had come up through the ranks and become an "engineer of aroma." Before I was given this honorable position, I had spent many months cleaning test tubes. It was important work as well.

No residue was safe from my strong action and technique. I was well schooled from my chemistry degree, and it soon became clear to my supervisor that I had done much more than just memorize every element on the periodic table.

The work of the lab was to manufacture scents, but not perfumes. Our tinctures were used when something needed to smell like what it was not. It was fascinating but strange work. For example, agents from the KGB would come to us when they needed to smell like residents from places where they were on assignment. You may not know someone from Leningrad has a different odor than someone from the Balkans or Siberia. Foreign lands as well were in our beakers and crucibles. Armenia, China, or France. We studied the eating, dressing, and lovemaking to give the agents the perfect cover, so no sniffing police dogs would discover their identity. Later on our work became top secret when the KGB needed to have a place to store dangerous chemicals and vaccines, products of military domination. The Soviet Army had their weapons, and we were to disguise them with the sweetest of aromas. Blackberry, amber, rose, and more.

Anyway, I saved some of the bras to sell in America, and the toilet tissue I left with my mother. The nurse slipped the bras under her desk and gave me an unenthusiastic nod with raised eyebrows.

"Have a pleasant journey," she mumbled.

I walked out onto Lermontovsky Prospekt, making my way toward Nevsky, where capitalism had haphazardly taken hold. Hundreds of billboards above the buildings along the main thoroughfare broke up the sky like an unfinished jigsaw puzzle. Blocking my view of St. Isaac's Cathedral was a giant woman's hand holding a freshly brewed cup of steaming black coffee.

* * *

I remember when our city was Leningrad—before it was once again St. Petersburg, as in the time of the czars—banners of our leaders decorated the same buildings. Walking to school one day, when I was about twelve, I stopped to watch as four workers hung an enormous poster of Stalin that filled the entire side of a building near the Fontanka Canal. Prominent in the foreground was our venerable leader, Secretary General Stalin, immaculately groomed, proud in his uniform, and behind him a hydroelectric plant. His salt-and-pepper hair was brushed back off his high forehead. Thick, lustrous eyebrows accentuated that smooth and unshakable brow. His almond-shaped hazel eyes gazed in a direction slightly to the painting's left, but more prominently out, to the future he saw for us. His perfectly tailored gray wool uniform was decorated with gold epaulets on the shoulders, red stripes on each side of the collar, and a gold star hanging from a crimson ribbon bar, pinned just above his left chest pocket that had a buttonless, double-stitched curved flap. It is a tricky piece of tailoring, if you've ever tried to sew.

I felt so much pride watching the poster unfurl down the side of the building; I was breathing heavily, my eyes liquid with emotion. Now that I thought of it, that image of Stalin must have brought up my first romantic feelings toward a man. My heart beat strongly under my heavy knit sweater, and through clogged nostrils I took sharp breaths as the tears streamed down my cheeks. I could not pull myself away. I wanted to live his vision. His hands proudly held a proclamation declaring the Soviet Union's economic and scientific superiority. All I wanted was for those hands to caress my face and for those arms to hold me next to him. I imagined myself in the poster, with his arm around my shoulder as we both looked out on the future, with the rushing water of the hydroelectric plant behind us, the power of Mother Russia clear in her generous natural resources, brilliant leadership, and worshipful youth.

There was a humility in Stalin's image that added to my infatuation. Behind him a red flag unfurled and framed his broad shoulders, and across the top of the poster the words of Lenin were inscribed on a field of red: "Communism is Soviet power plus the electrification of the entire country." Stalin was doing all the work, but he still deferred to Lenin, and I loved him for that even more.

The school's first bell disrupted my trance. I'd forgotten where I was meant to be.

"Good-bye, Stalina," Stalin spoke from the poster. "Go to your classes; I'll wait here for you. Go now—study hard and be a good young Communist."

I sat down at my desk, still in a state of shock, looking around at my classmates to see if they noticed how I'd changed. No one could know the fire in my heart. Olga was busy fixing the ribbon in Amalia's hair, and Yuri, the class comedian, was performing his version of *Swan Lake* when our teacher, Mrs. Tolga, scolded him mid pirouette and sent him to sit in the back even though we all could see he made her laugh along with the rest of us.

The class settled, and all was quiet except for the crack of our opening notebooks. The lesson on the board in bold block letters read: WRITE A POEM ABOUT HOW COMMUNISM HELPS ONE AND ALL.

I could only keep thinking, "Stalin spoke to me—he spoke to me."

"Take me, I'm yours," I whispered and scribbled over and over in my notebook. On another page I drew a copy of the poster, this time including myself at Stalin's side, our collective gaze seeing past the streets and buildings of Leningrad to the fields and factories soon to be nourished with our country's newfound power and wealth. My love was so new, and myself and my country so terribly naïve.

* * *

Now, almost fifty years later, I looked above the billboard advertisement for imported coffee and watched as the clouds moved toward Finland. The next day I would be in a plane passing through similar clouds on my way to America.

As I continued home, I made up a song with the directions Amalia had sent me to her home in Connecticut, USA. I sang them with a boogie-woogie beat and swayed my hips inside my long wool coat.

St. Petersburg to Moscow-ca-ca-COW!
Moscow, Kennedy, Port Authori-TAY!
Bus to Hartford, three hours' ride,
45 Star Lane, the taxi will drive!

As I walked through the streets, the buildings loomed, and I imagined their dismay regarding my departure.

The doorways, windows, and back alleys whispered behind my back, "How dare you leave us after all we've been through."

I answered, "You can't hold me anymore. There is nothing for me here. America wants me."

I touched the sides of the buildings and felt every crack and bump in the sidewalks and cobbled streets. This brokenhearted city would have to survive without me. It would be best for both of us. I tried to explain.

"I do love you, but it's not practical for us to be together."

"That's a lame excuse, Stalina," the sewer gate sputtered up at me.

I stomped my foot on the grating and said, "Leave me be. You know nothing!"

I turned a corner onto St. Isaac's Square. The sun reflected off the cathedral's golden dome. It was a beautiful sight to behold. I unbuttoned my coat to let the sun warm my chest. The angels surrounding the dome held torches that would be lit again for the first time in forty years that Easter. Silenced for so long, they took this opportunity to speak their minds.

"Sweet Stalina, don't leave us," they sang down to St. Isaac's Square.

"I love you, but don't cross me now. Everything has changed. I can't stay," I tried to explain again.

"Dirty Jew!" one of the angels screamed.

"Who speaks like a Cossack?" I wanted to know.

"Jew. Jew. Jew. Always a Jew!" they kept chanting.

I pulled my fur hat down over my ears and made my way home, where my bag was already packed.

Chapter Three: Stamped in Red

Amalia had written to me, "Bring something to remember home. Bring something to sell, and wear as much clothing as possible on the plane. You want to have space in your bag for anything to be used for commerce, to sell or barter. It is part of survival in America. Fly to Moscow from Petersburg. The flight from Moscow to US will cost less, even with the connection."

At the airport outside Petersburg the next day, the customs officer found my packing job quite amusing, commenting, "Looks like you need an engineer's degree to pack a bag like this."

"My degree is in chemistry. It is all about how things in the universe fit together, like a well-packed valise."

"Your universe is a curious place," he said as he ran his fingers along the top of the bras I had packed.

He touched everything in my bag. Under each of his fingernails was a line of black dirt collected from digging into other people's possessions. I had systematically packed my double-strapped leather valise with the twenty-four brassieres, sizes 75B to 85DD. Sized in our metric system, I hoped these undergarments would make American ladies feel grand; 34B to 44DD is otherwise unimpressive. I used several of the larger sized bras to protect my collection of porcelain cats. The oldest one, a Siamese, was a present from Olga for my ninth birthday. Underneath the cats I had packed my father's copy of *Julius Caesar*, his favorite play, and a leather-bound copy of Lewis Carroll's *Through the Looking Glass*, which he read to me every year on my birthday when I was young. A photo album with pictures of my family and friends lay at the bottom of the bag, along with framed photos of my grandparents cushioned by my grandmother's fur hat and gloves. I'd heard the American winters were bad—not as cold as Leningrad, but very wet. Poetry books by Anna Akhmatova had stockings and other undergarments wrapped around them. Into five pairs of socks I packed ten Russian *matryoshka* dolls, which I understood to be popular in America. I find them disturbing, as they show how easily a woman can be reduced to practically nothing. On top I laid my lab coat, which I'd received as a gift from Trofim, my chemistry professor from university. My lover.

The customs man read my name on the passport. "Stalina, that's a lovely name."

He obviously did not go to school with me. My fellow students would belittle me about my name. They would say, "Take another name, Stalina. How about Lotte or Anna or Tatiana? Millions died under Stalin. You are not his namesake anymore. Take this monster away from your life."

"I will never change it," I told them. "My name is our past."

Perhaps this customs officer was a supporter of Stalin. There are those who wish for a return to Stalinism, and to honor the general for stopping the Nazis. In Petersburg today a small group stands in front of the Grostiny Dvor department store on Nevsky Prospekt with sandwich boards and petitions disseminating information for their cause. Occasionally an argument erupts between them and passersby, but in general they are just thought to be crazy and are whispered about in the cafés.

I passed him my papers. There are no lies on my passport. A capital letter *J* stamped in the lower left corner indicates I am a Jew. When I left, the government made it easy for Jews, especially an oldie like me, to leave. The customs inspector handed back my passport and made a slow, deliberate stroke with his forefinger along the top of my hand. I took my bag and smiled out of relief at passing the inspection. As I walked through the gate, I felt his stare on my heavily padded behind swinging from side to side like a cushion-covered pendulum.

I did not sleep and mostly cried during the twelve-hour flight to America. The clouds surrounded us like steam at my local banya. Instead of glistening bodies revealed in the breaks of heavy mist, I saw a landscape of clouds and ice-capped mountains as we crossed over Finland and then Greenland, where the sun's light was tippling off the waves of the Atlantic. When we lost the sun and the moon rose, the dark waters looked like scores of crystal chandeliers lighting our way. The sun had come up when we left Petersburg, and I saw it rise again as we passed over an island the stewardess called Prince Edward. While in the air, I sorted through memories and divided them like the test tubes I once cleaned in the lab. Long, short, cracked, hard to see through, lined with residue, all dropped into the washbasin of my brain, bobbing to the surface when a path was made clear, or simply pulled up from below with a snap of my rubber-gloved hand.

* * *

Seeing a glimpse of the ocean's waves through the clouds made me think of how I used to swim in the Gulf of Finland with my mother just a few years before I left Russia. The doctors said it was the best therapy for her dementia.

"The cold water will awaken the senses and stimulate the organs. Her blood will flow more readily. It's all about blood flow," they would say.

My mother had been a member of a water ballet collective in her youth and consequently swam beautifully. I loved to watch her swim and tried to imitate her curved arms and the precise entry of her fingertips into the water. On one of our regular Sunday swims, a family secret was revealed.

That day Mother came up for air after a long time underwater and announced, "Swimming makes me think of Maxim."

Maxim was my uncle.

She continued, "Maxim kissed me underwater."

I thought she was confused. "Don't you mean Father kissed you?"

"No! Kisses were from Maxim. We kissed so long we had no air; he emptied the last drop of air into my lungs."

"You almost drowned?"

"We bobbed to the surface, and I breathed the air back into his lungs."

"What about Father?"

My mother replied, "Your father let me have the pleasure I did not have with him."

"With his brother?"

"He's not your uncle." She was annoyed as if I should have known.

As we both treaded water, a seagull landed near us. The bird screeched at a piece of sodden bread floating by and grabbed it in his beak. Another bird swooped down and stole it out of his mouth. The first gull did not pursue his foe. Instead, he floated past us and let out a feeble screech to no one in particular.

"How spineless," I thought. That gull reminded me of my father, who would stay home writing and drinking when my mother and Maxim would go out together. After a couple of years, he was only drinking and never wrote anything new. He would obsessively read and reread his published poems and essays, pacing up and down our room holding the book or journal in front of him and taking a pen from behind his ear to make the changes. He wrote about vodka as a metaphor for oppressive government. Many of his poems were in English. His supporters would learn them and deliver his words through the underground to publishers outside Russia. I memorized all his poems. This was a typical practice to save the writings of our country's poets. On paper their work could easily be lost, destroyed, or sent to the authorities. Like this one:

Stalin demands we drink his vodka.
Why should he be everyone's doctor?
Perish the thought if you drank sangria,
Cover your ears to block his logorrhea.
Our future will rise like a glass filled with
Schnapps, port, or rye.
Your choice, your high,
While the others fall blind, no future, no time.

He inspired other writers to write what was on their minds, while he became more and more crippled by the loss of freedom for words and humor. It was to him the height of cruelty. At the end of the night, the liquor would be gone and the pages were unintelligible.

* * *

After going through some unexpected turbulence, the plane landed safely in New York City on September 30, 1991. That was when my strange new life began.

Chapter Four: Port Authori-TAY

Kennedy Airport is all about moving things. Airplanes, luggage, people, money, coffee, donuts. Bleary-eyed and swollen from the trip, I welcomed the moving sidewalk and slowly drifted forward. The people who walked along the outside concrete sidewalk were faster than the motorized one. With some relief to my swollen ankles, I moved closer to the real America. People stood along the corridors waiting and straining to see all the arriving passengers. A man clutched a photograph in one hand and a straw hat in the other. A family of six, everyone exactly the same height and not very tall, bobbed up and down in a huddle like a pack of prairie dogs. At the luggage transport, I spotted the double straps of my satchel rounding the curve and pushed through the crowd to grab the worn leather handles. A line formed for customs. Soon it was my turn. The officer did not flirt with me this time, but he did look me straight in the eye.

"Are you here on business or pleasure?" he asked.

"I'm here for good."

"Business or pleasure?"

"To stay."

"Good for you, business or pleasure?" He was all business and a bit annoyed.

"I hope pleasure."

"OK, pleasure it will be. Step back, please."

As he opened my bag, I could smell the thick, damp air from the plaster walls of my Petersburg apartment in the liberated molecules. The customs officer did not appear to notice. The name on the tag on his pocket read Sgt. Green. In Russian green is *zilliony*. His name at home would be Sergeant Zilliony. I liked that better than Green. The first sign of spring at winter's end when the flowers force themselves through the softening earth—*zilliony*. In America the color green is about money, greed, and envy.

He opened my photo album and turned it over. A dried bouquet fell out from between the pages. Oh, Trofim. He had given me the flowers with the lab coat at my graduation in Vilnius. He was my professor of physics and chemistry. He was brilliant in both, ran the Young Scientists Club, and was asked to make a speech at the graduation ceremony. Everyone envied my position as his assistant. We spent a lot of time side by side over experiments, but never touched. When his job ended in Vilnius, he was sent to the State University of Leningrad. I was returning home after my studies and was thrilled he would be there. When his family did not follow him to Leningrad for several months, we could not help ourselves.

The officer held up the flattened bouquet and asked, "You have pansies in Russia?"

"Yes, we grow many flowers, but those are not pansies. I believe they are violets."

"Oh, a horticulturist, well isn't that nice."

"A chemist, actually. I just like flowers."

Sergeant Zilliony prodded at the brassieres, upsetting many more of the precious particles from home. All the remnants of my Russia were being sucked through a black hole in this foreign atmosphere.

"Welcome to America. Good luck," the customs officer said as he closed my bag.

"*Do svidaniya*," I replied, but Sergeant Green had already moved on to the next foreigners and did not acknowledge my good-bye.

Next in line were a group of Italians with many suitcases and cardboard boxes. The officer watched as they lifted everything onto his examination table. Another uniformed person pointed me in the direction of yet another uniform. There my passport was scrutinized by a woman behind a high counter. I had to stand on the tips of my toes to see her. It felt good to stretch my ankles. She looked at me sideways.

"You are here to stay?"

"Yes."

She said nothing and just stamped my passport. That was it. It was official—I was in America.

I went through double metal swinging doors, and on the other side, several men dressed in black pants and white shirts were holding signs with handwritten names. They spoke Russian.

"My son is going to engineering school."

"Did you file for Social Security?"

"I am not eligible."

"Take a class at the college."

"Pottery, perhaps?"

They laughed and displayed their signs overhead as the area started to fill with people. I panicked for a moment hearing them speak Russian. Had I gotten on the wrong plane? No, I was here. The sign said "Welcome to the United States of America" in several alphabets, including Cyrillic. The tall glass windows, the smell of coffee and fried dough, and the smiling, toothy grins of the people in posters screamed *America*. When I finally stepped out into the bright, hot day and took a deep breath and tasted the steel-spiced air, I realized I was very far from home. The airport's harsh smells, mixed with glaring sun at the curbside, made me wince. I sang my little song for comfort.

St. Petersburg to Moscow-ca-ca-COW!

Moscow, Kennedy, Port Authori-tay!

Excited and nervous, I wanted to do a little dance, but I managed to control my enthusiasm. I was in America and had to get to Port Authority. Port—I had some port once, and I enjoyed it very much. Authority—in the Soviet Union, it always made me suspicious. All the English words swimming before my eyes gave me vertigo. I tilted my head down between my knees to stop the spinning, and when I stood up and opened my eyes, in front of me was a bus with the name of my destination written on a sign across the top of its window. It was my first "lucky break" in America. I found a seat, and when the motor started rumbling, the diesel fumes reminded me of home. I clutched my precious valise on my lap. There were roads being built and many hotels along the route to Port Authority. The traffic was moving toward a skyline I had only seen in pictures. The man sitting next to me had a leg that twitched, and his suit smelled of oranges. He held his leg to stop it from bouncing up and down. He smiled at me, but I could not find a smile on my face yet—I was too nervous. I kept thinking of my song:

Bus to Hartford, three hours' ride,
45 Star Lane, the taxi will drive.

"Breathe, Stalina, breathe," my father's voice whispered to me from sometime long ago. I missed him and started to relax.

Chapter Five: Liberty

Once at Port Authority, I had two hours before the next bus was leaving for Hartford, Connecticut. Out of the bus I touched the concrete and felt the ground shaking. I stood frozen, holding tightly to my bag. The bus driver was helping people get their luggage. He saw my hesitation to move.

"Don't worry, ma'am, it's the subway you're feeling. The Eighth Avenue IND runs right under our feet."

"In Russia our metro is deep, deep underground."

"Go right through that door, ma'am. You have arrived in New York City."

The bus terminal was very different from the airport. It was as if nothing was moving. Many people were wearing dark clothes and were slumped in corners and against the walls. I made my way quickly past staring eyes to get outdoors to breathe some air. *Breathe, Stalina, breathe.* The smell of this place was not sweet, and it was rather harsh on my newly arrived senses. I found the stairway up. It was one of those that should move—an escalator. This one did not move. I stepped over a gentleman to begin my climb up to the street. Overhead there were beams with words printed on them. Each beam had another word. A poem on a beam. On the first beam it said *OVERSLEPT*, then the next had

WORN-OUT, and then seven more to complete the unhappy reprise:

IF TARDY
GET LAID OFF
WHY WORRY?
WHY THE GRIEF?
JUST GO BACK
DO IT OVER
AND OVER AGAIN

The Port Authority had a sadness to it that was strangely comforting. It was not just in Russia that people had hard times. I was being shown the real America. Clutching my valise, I went through the glass doors to a very noisy avenue. The street in front of the building was torn apart, and a deep hole made the traffic stop. It sounded as if every horn was sounding from every car. There were workers in the hole, and I could see the tops of their yellow hard hats bobbing as they threw dirt over their shoulders with shovels. I turned the corner and practically tripped over the spike-heeled shoes of a very tall woman with bony legs in fishnet tights and a skirt that came up to my nose. Her black hair stuck straight into the air like the sharp tips on barbed wire. It was obviously a wig.

I pulled back and said, "Pardon me."

She did not say a word as she crossed her long leg behind her and leaned against the wall. Another woman wearing a tight-fitting dress made of bright green satin tapped her shoulder and asked for a cigarette. Prostitutes. Again I see America is much like Russia. Only our ladies of the street are not so old and hard. As I cleared away from their sidewalk space and stepped toward the curb, I saw the Christ Almighty Savior Church on Forty-second Street. The angels over the arched doorway were like those on top of St. Isaac's. Next door to the church was a storefront with "Rosalinda the Psychic" painted across the window. I crossed the street to get a closer look.

The palm reader, a blond, looked like an old woman as she sat, tired and slumped in a chair. As I stood in front of the window, she beckoned me to come inside. Her hands were smooth with no wrinkles. I saw she was younger than me, perhaps forty or even younger, but even this age she wore with a heavy burden. I did not hesitate to go inside. With the streets busy and crowded, I was glad for the special attention. She stood and showed me to a white plastic chair next to a table with a crystal ball cradled in the claw of an eagle. A travel poster of a cathedral in Madrid was on the wall above where she wanted me to sit. As she turned and motioned to the chair, she moved like a dancer of flamenco. There was a curtain closing off the back, and from behind I could smell onions being cooked in oil. She sat and leaned her head down to arrange the cards and figurines on the table. She clearly needed to color her hair. The black roots at her scalp would have offended Olga, who despised very much incompetent dye jobs.

"Please relax; you look tired. My name is Frederica; my mother was Rosalinda," she explained before I asked. She took my hand.

"I am Sta—"

She stopped me. "No, don't tell me. Please show me the photographs you are carrying in your purse."

I was impressed by her clairvoyance. How could she have known I always carry family pictures? She looked through them.

"Tell me about the people in this picture."

She was asking about the photograph taken on the porch of our dacha outside Leningrad, taken in the days after the Great Patriotic War (or if you are not Russian, World War II).

"That is Amalia and me. We were childhood friends, and now I have come here to stay with her in Connecticut, USA."

"Tell me more."

I told Frederica how when we were growing up, of all my friends, Amalia had the most fascinating look. I loved how her front teeth came forward with a slight overbite, and I was full of awe because of the red birthmark that covered half her face. The makeup she applied to conceal the mark was the color of red clay and made her look very exotic. With her hair pulled back, she reminded me of the Indians riding horses in the Westerns we saw at the cinema on Saturdays when we were eleven years old. Every morning she applied makeup to her face, but by the time the sun was going down, it would fade, and the redness would be like a half mask across the left side of her face. In the summer evenings, Amalia and I would sit with my grandparents on the porch playing cards. When the sun had gone behind the house, my grandfather would light the lantern, and we would keep playing until my mother called us in for baths and bed. In the attic room where we slept, we would talk until all hours about movie stars and how we would style our hair for school in the fall. In the morning Amalia always got up first. I would hear her in the bathroom putting on her foundation and powder like her mother had taught her. I pretended to sleep until she finished and then met her downstairs. We would be the only ones awake.

"Do you want to hear all about this?" I asked Frederica.

"She is connected to your future. I want to hear everything."

I continued to tell her how in the morning Amalia would prepare two bowls of fresh plums and cream, our favorite secret breakfast together. Amalia taught me how to kiss on those mornings. Frederica shifted my palm in her warm, chubby hands with rings on every finger.

"Continue," she said.

"Amalia would say, 'Watch me, Stalina. This is the way it's done.' After peeling back the skin of the plum and revealing its brown and purple flesh, she would wet her lips. 'Remember, don't tense—let them relax, feel full. Your lips must be soft and determined at the same time.' Lifting a plum from the bowl, she would bring it toward her lips and lean in a little over the cream. Her lips and the plum became one."

I explained how we would continue to eat in silence, bobbing the peeled plums, watching the morning sunlight bounce off our spoons onto the walls. Karlik and Meeyassa, my two cats who would be called Little One and Meat in English, swatted at the flickerings along the top of the refrigerator. One cat would swipe and hit the other. Timid Meat would jump down first and hiss back up at Little One and go under my chair, where I always put the bowl of unfinished cream.

As I spoke, Frederica continued to look at my left palm. With a long, sharp fingernail she traced the lines in my hand. Her black nail polish was peeling. The sunlight was streaking in a slant through the front window, hitting her heavily made-up eyes. Flecks of mascara were clumped on her lashes, and her lips were painted deep purple, the same color as the plums. The lipstick had seeped into the age lines around her mouth like the canals that split off the Neva River at home.

Frederica spoke as if a vision had come to her. "You are on a long journey."

This clairvoyance did not impress me. After all, I had not slept in twenty-four hours, my eyes were heavy, I had my valise packed full at my side, and even though I speak English with good confidence, my accent is quite thick. She could tell I was not very impressed, so she held both my palms in her hands and stared at them.

"Are you comfortable hearing about past lives?" she asked.

I said yes, not because I believe in life after death, but I still had forty minutes before my bus would leave, and I was curious.

"You were in a desperate situation because of your religion."

"Once a Jew, always a Jew," I said, laughing. "Let my people go? Inquisition? Would you like me to continue?"

She was serious.

"One of those. Your safety was compromised, and you were forced to take your four children away, which ended in great tragedy. There were deaths. Your husband was not of your religion, so he was safe. At the time, your relationship was one of much dependency. That all fell apart, and you never recovered."

For some reason I keep getting sent back as a Jew.

"'You, you, always a Jew,' the angels yelled down at me from St. Isaac's Cathedral before I left Russia," I told her.

"Angels, that's good. They don't hate Jews—they're just doing someone else's bidding."

"Could have fooled me," I said under my breath.

"Please may I see the other pictures?" she asked.

I pulled out the pictures of my grandmother, our neighbors, my mother, father, and Trofim.

At that moment an official car with a siren blaring and lights flashing pulled up out front. It was the police, and two officers got out and came into Frederica's salon.

"We have a warrant for the arrest of Anthony Hermona," one of the officers announced.

I froze. I did not want to be part of anything illegal during my first hours in America. Frederica said nothing, just indicated with her eyes and a tilt of her head to the curtain at the back of the room. The officers went through, and there was a scuffle in the back. A few moments later a young man with dark, oily hair and sweat stains at his armpits was led away in handcuffs. Frederica was silent until the police had driven away. I stared at a moving waterfall in a frame that was also a clock. It was three o'clock. I waited for Frederica to say something.

"He's my nephew. He sold cocaine to the wrong people. They'll let him out in a week. I told the police he knew a lot. Now they'll watch out for my store. Sorry for the disturbance."

She gave her nephew to the police! I realized that America is more like Russia than I imagined, only there the police would never have stopped at the door. The clock now said five after three.

"My bus is leaving for Hartford soon. I must be going," I explained as I stood to leave.

"There were betrayals among these people," she said, giving me back the pictures.

"Betrayals? It was common," I responded.

"You were not the one betrayed. But you will be. Five dollars, please," she said.

"There is a Russian saying that goes, 'Being the daughter of the betrayed is like having alcoholic parents. You may end up becoming a bartender.' Why five dollars? The sign says three."

"You are too stuck in your past, and that was the old sign."

"I have to get on a bus to Hartford—that's the future."

I handed her five dollars. Amalia had sent me a stack of five-dollar bills so I would not have to change money right away. The rubles I took from Russia were stuffed inside the hollow centers of my porcelain cats protected by the brassieres. Months later I would wish it had been the cats protecting the brassieres.

Frederica scrutinized the five-dollar bill in the sunlight. As I left, she pulled a cigarette from behind her ear and placed my money inside her brassiere. She wore a tight-fitting black sweater that showed off her sagging but plentiful breasts. She stood in stockinged feet on the plastic fake grass mat in front of her store. Through her black opaque stockings I could see her toes were painted red and she had a bunion on her left foot. She drew loudly on her cigarette and exhaled even louder. A sign of an addict, I could tell. I walked to the corner and went inside the Port Authority. The bus was waiting at gate fifteen.

The bus driver said, "Let me put your bag under here," indicating somewhere deep in the belly of the bus.

"No, thank you," I replied.

"Sup to you," he said.

English was still often baffling to me. I wondered what "sup" meant, but I did not dare ask as the bus driver was busy with the next passengers.

The seats were soft, the bus dark, and the diesel fumes once again made me feel cozy and relaxed. As the bus rumbled out of the depot into the narrow streets, I could barely see any sky between the tall buildings. We went into a tunnel, and in the darkness I fell into the exhaustion of my journey and slept. In my dreams, I was still in Russia.

* * *

I was deep in a Russian forest and could hear, but could not see, someone chopping down a tree. I was nervous for the person chopping, as if the tree was going to fall on them. Eventually after much effort, the woodsman felled the tree. I could see through the clearing that it was my grandfather. He was holding up his right hand, showing a mangled index finger. In his youth it was common for young men to chop off their trigger fingers or shoot wax into their leg veins to make them varicose to escape serving in the czar's army. My grandfather's finger was mangled in real life, but I never knew how it happened. A flash went off in the dream—a spy wearing a black hood photographed my grandfather burying the top joint of his finger.

* * *

I woke, startled. My mouth had dropped open, and my tongue was parched. I looked at the watch of the man sitting next to me and saw that it was almost six o'clock. I had slept for a long time, and in order to see where I was, I read the signs on the stores as the bus sped by.

Arturo's Haircuts—Best in Hartford—Only $5

The bus stopped at a traffic light. My legs were numb from the weight of my bag.

"Prroh, prroh, prroh…" the man next to me started to splutter. He was dreaming and sounded like a motorboat engine struggling to start. I held tightly onto my bag.

"Prrr…prognosis!" came out loud and clear. His breath smelled of sour milk. He startled himself awake, sat up, and stared directly at me.

"You were having a dream?" I said.

"I said something?" he asked.

"You said 'prognosis,'" I replied.

"Strange—sorry to disturb you."

"Not a problem."

"I can't remember what I was dreaming."

The wisps of brown hair on his head were going every which way. He held his glasses in his hand and had to squint to see me.

"Are you a doctor?" I asked.

He put his glasses on. The lenses were thick and tinted blue. He was round in his belly and had a young cherub face. He looked much friendlier now that his mouth was closed.

"No. Why? Oh, I said 'prognosis.' I remember now—it was a dream about having a terrible illness."

"I hope that is not the case," I added.

"No, I'm fine. I watch too many of those hospital shows on television. I like your accent."

"I'm Russian."

The bus started moving again. We passed more signs.

Pete's-A-Place: Hartford's First Sicilian Pizza

"Pete's-A-Place, Pete's-A, piz-za—that's funny," I said to my neighbor.

"You have pizza in Russia?" he asked.

"Yes, we enjoy it very much."

Freddy's Glass Eye Emporium—Buy and Sell Connecticut

I hope never to need one of those.

Berlin Sneaker Circus

The bus turned onto Windsor Avenue. We passed motel after motel.

Route Five Pay and Stay

Amalia had written me about these places.

Windsor Castle Motel

She was a dispatcher for the Majik Cleaning Agency of Hartford. She mentioned that they often hired maids to clean the rooms, and she would try to get me a job at one of them. At first I thought I would easily get a job in my field of science, but I quickly learned that was not going to happen. I needed to work. I went to several testing labs for hospitals. Amalia suggested they would need someone with my training. But in order to work for these places, I would need certification from a school in America. They are very particular about how samples taken for testing are handled and disposed. All new employees are required to work with the most contagious materials. I was not impressed with the conditions, nor did I have time or money to go to school. And on top of that, the idea of working with dangerous waste was not what I wanted for my life here. I know it is important work, but it felt good to leave at least some of my past behind me. Amalia understood, and soon after my arrival she told me of a cleaning position available at the final motel the bus had passed. Plain, honest work. The Liberty Motel. I liked the name. It was the reason I was here. The bus was just minutes from the Hartford depot. My neighbor had fallen back to sleep and was snoring loudly.

The last lab where I worked in Russia kept me on because of the hazardous materials they were storing. Anthrax and smallpox were their specialty. It was dangerous to work around these things, but as a Jew I was very dependent on the ebb and flow of who was in charge, so in order to keep my job I was willing to work under conditions that many others would refuse. "Your sickle must rest silently," the head of the lab would say. That was no issue for me.

But in Connecticut, just before the Christmas holiday in 1991, I was very pleased when Amalia organized a job for this Jew at the Liberty Motel a few weeks after I arrived in Hartford, USA. At first, Mr. Suri, the manager and owner, resisted hiring me because he wanted someone younger.

"It's not because you're Jewish, he just prefers younger employees," Amalia assured me.

She told me how the last maid he hired, a woman my age, was caught giving favors to a customer in the laundry room.

"I'm trying to run a legitimate business here. Don't send me any more of your hard cases," he told Amalia.

"I have someone perfect, Mr. Suri. She has dignity. We were childhood friends. Her English is excellent. Stalina will be a great asset to your establishment," she told him. "Trust me."

Chapter Six: Liberty Motel, Rooms for the Imaginative

One of the first things I noticed about the motel was that Mr. Suri hung postcards of the Statue of Liberty, his favorite tourist site, over the front desk. There was one picture of Miss Liberty in profile that reminded me of my mother. A strong jaw, full lips, and a nose that came straight down from her forehead. On the back of the postcard it explained that the spikes of her crown represent the seven seas and seven continents. I would like to visit her one day. It looks like a lovely spot, and you can walk all the way up inside her. She has a crown like a queen, even though there is no royalty here.

After working there for a few months, I learned the Liberty Motel is also something of an attraction. Known in the business as a "short-stay" establishment, it's a place for lovers in need of privacy. Prostitutes and politicians, traveling salespeople, truckers, and teenagers living at home all frequent the hotel. Money flows easily through such hands. Sometimes it's all in single-dollar bills. Sixteen dollars and fifty cents per hour paid up front. I treat everyone the same, underworld and *overworld*. But it's not always easy to do. Once a prostitute was so badly beaten that I wanted to call an ambulance, but she refused to go to the hospital. I took care of her, and when I removed the ice pack from her swollen eyes and cleaned her makeup, it was only then I realized she was just a girl, sixteen, seventeen. Times like that bring sorrow to my day. But it's not always like that, not even often.

Stained carpet, broken side tables, and stale smells from cigarettes and alcohol were the basic decor of the rooms when I first started working here. One day I asked Mr. Suri if he would let me redecorate the rooms. "What's wrong with them?" he protested. "There is a heart-shaped Jacuzzi in one room that cost me five hundred dollars."

"Yes, and when people leave that room, they tell me how much they like it," I patiently explained.

"Stalina, let's leave it at that."

"I can make beautiful rooms."

"No."

"Sixty dollars per room."

"No."

"Think of the motel sign." I'd thought about the name before presenting the idea. "Liberty Motel, Rooms for the Imaginative."

"What do you mean, imaginative?" he asked.

"I will make a different fantasy setting for each room for only three hundred and sixty total dollars. Sixty dollars per room."

"Three hundred and sixty dollars. That's only twenty-two short-stay hours, less than one day," he said and smoothed the corners of his mustache.

Mr. Suri was smart and good at math, and I'd noticed that he played with his mustache when he was about to agree to something. About forty years of age or so, he had the long, graceful hands of a pianist, and in profile he reminded me of that handsome actor Omar Sharif. He came here eight years ago from India with his wife, their young son, Chander, who was now ten, and his brother Garson. An uncle died and left them the motel. Mr. Suri's wife left him for another man about a year after they moved here. I had never seen her. She moved to New Mexico with the child. Amalia told me this much. Mr. Suri had pictures of his son dressed as a cowboy in the office, but none of the boy's mother. I think he was depressed because sometimes he sat alone under the pine trees in front of the motel drawing with a stick in the dirt. He was quiet and did not laugh very often. Garson I hardly ever saw. Whenever they talked on the phone, I heard much stress in Mr. Suri's voice. Garson was younger than Mr. Suri and had a daughter who worked here at the motel. Mara was the niece; she was seventeen and very lazy when it came to her job of cleaning the rooms. Mr. Suri thought she was saving money to go to college, but I knew she planned to run off with her boyfriend. I'd heard conversations they had over the intercom in the linen room.

Mr. Suri finally agreed to my idea.

"I'll let you do two rooms, and then we'll see. Don't touch my heart-shaped tub."

He was very fond of this red tub.

"My first room will be called 'Gazebo in a Rainstorm,'" I announced.

"I like gazebos," he replied.

I had seen a gazebo in a magazine called *House and Garden*. I get much of my inspiration for my room designs from the pictures in American magazines. *Good Housekeeping, Travel and Leisure, Women's Day*.

Then he surprised me by saying, "Since Mara has been helping with the cleaning, I want you to take a shift at the front desk."

Usually Mr. Suri or his brother managed that part of the business because of the money. The motel operates twenty-four hours a day. The customers' visits must be timed correctly, and everyone gets a fifteen-minute warning from the front desk phone. I felt moved by Mr. Suri's trust and confidence. In addition to my respect for Mr. Suri—you could say my affection—I was glad to be a part of making his business successful. The business of business interests me very much. I might be older than Mr. Suri by a number of years, but I could still swing my hips and offer compliments to his nature when it helped to make our business run smoothly. Russian women know how to get what they want: no distractions, no destruction.

"I'd like you to do the morning shift. Garson has agreed."

"Eight a.m. to…?"

"Just till four p.m. My brother and I will split the evening and overnight shifts."

"I can work on my room designs while I'm at the front desk."

"As long as you keep everything straight."

"Yes sir. At your service, Mr. Suri."

It made him uncomfortable when I called him sir, but he smiled and offered me the seat at the front desk in the office. It felt as if I were receiving an important award.

"I have to go to Hartford to get a permit for the septic system," he informed me.

He winked at me as he turned to go outside.

"Room five has twenty minutes left. They'll need a warning soon," he added.

The March wind blew across the driveway and into the pine trees as he drove away in his large, gold Delta '88. I tidied up the front desk and then made my call to room number five. The phone rang four times.

"Hmm, huh?" a female voice responded.

"Fifteen minutes," I answered.

There was no further discussion. We hung up simultaneously. I embraced my new assignment with the fervor of a flag bearer at a May Day parade in Moscow.

Chapter Seven: My Father

Two weeks later, I unveiled room number one, "Gazebo in a Rainstorm," to Mr. Suri. He was very impressed. Room number two had become the "Roller Coaster Fun Park." There had been much activity at the motel and much gossip up and down Windsor Avenue about these rooms. The other motels were feeling the competition and had started to add their own attractions. The Flamingo's sign read "Sun Lamps in Every Room," the Windsor Castle added "Feel Like Royalty in Our Rooms," and the Route Five Pay and Stay advertised "Lunch Hour Specials."

Capitalism was exciting, even with its flaws. To be positioned on top was a complicated goal for a Russian soul. I understood better now my childhood friend, Nadia, who was singular in her desire to compete and succeed above all her peers. She had a passion to possess and control in the face of any obstacle. When we were children she was always judging, comparing, and pushing us out of the way. She always wanted to seem superior and boasted about everything. I would always try to counter her attempts to make us feel inferior. Whether we were ten, twelve, or twenty, it was always pretty much the same. Here is a typical conversation, word for word.

"My father makes more money than your father."

"Yes, Nadia, he does," I said. Her father was a baker and a well-paid informant for the NKVD.

"My house has more windows than yours."

"Big deal. More cleaning for your mother."

"My hair is straighter and shinier than yours," she would say, flipping her long, straight, blond hair behind her shoulders.

"I like the wave in my hair," I replied.

"I have a sister."

"I have pity for her."

"My dog is more obedient than yours."

Making a judgment about my dog made me angry. Her miniature poodle, Trala, with the matted white hair and leaky pink eyes, may have been more cooperative than my strong-willed terrier, Pepe, but her dog was showy and obnoxious, just like her. My parents made me put up with Nadia and her dog.

"She lives right next door, she is smart, has good manners, and her family is well connected," my mother would say.

She was well mannered in front of the adults, but she treated her friends like servants. No wonder my dog Pepe bit her. Soon after that incident, when Nadia and I were seventeen, both Pepe and my father were gone.

* * *

Pepe had been gone for a month the day my father disappeared.

My mother lied. "They needed soldiers to fight the fascists. Your father agreed to go."

"When will he return?"

I asked the same question about Pepe. My mother's answer about dog and father was to light a cigarette.

Amalia later told me the truth.

"Your mother has no idea what he was arrested for, so she made up the fighting fascists story. There are no fascists to fight—we beat them all in the war," she said while we played cards.

"It's not a story. My father is a soldier," I responded.

"Your father is a writer."

"So?"

"Writers are the worst, and on top of that your father wears that ridiculous hat," she said, making a face and pulling her hands down over her ears.

My father wore a tight-fitting blue beret. He used to say it kept out the lies of his neighbors.

Amalia added, "And besides that silly hat, your dog bit Nadia."

"My father punished Pepe," I said, holding four aces, a jack, and a queen and king of hearts in my hand. "Amalia, I don't think you shuffled these cards very well."

"When was the last time your father published anything?"

"When he returns, he will write about the fighting," I said, holding the photograph of my father in my hand along with my playing cards.

"You're a duckling head," Amalia said and sneered from behind her cards.

"Don't call me names. Gin!" I said and put my cards down.

"Did you hear Nadia's dog Trala disappeared?" she said, turning the photograph of my father around to face her and tapping it with her finger.

"Who cares?" I said. "She and her dog can go to hell."

"Nice shovel he has there," she said, holding the photograph close to her face. "I did not know your father was a gardener. Your deal."

Chapter Eight: Makeovers

Life was so different at the Liberty Motel. I'll now take a moment to describe the décor of my room designs. With these "Rooms for the Imaginative" I hoped to bring happiness to our small part of the world here in Berlin, Connecticut, a little bit of green (and yes, concrete), easy to get to from all the converging highways that feed into the city of Hartford. Berlin was like a young sibling in a struggling family—the town waited for the castoffs from big brother Hartford. Everything in the town from the road signs to the picket fences around the tiny front yards looked tired and worn.

Upon entering room number one, you encountered a bed on a raised platform with a six-sided gazebo built around it. I called it the "bed-zebo." It had green ivy around the posts at the sides of the platform and thin strips of clear plastic attached to each of the six sides. With the air moving from the ceiling fan, the Mylar fluttered and gave the feeling of rain falling. Getting trapped in a gazebo during bad weather is very stimulating. Movies and novels are filled with such moments. Who wouldn't want it? I decorated the roof of the bed with wood shingles, but it was what you saw upon looking up from the bed that made this a very popular room. There were six triangular mirrors fitted into the top turrets in the roof. The reflections broke into six different views from anywhere in the bed. Even though I had only been in the bed alone, I still found the angles and broken views quite stimulating. The sides of the bed and the platform were covered with green plastic grass. It was the same stuff like the mat outside Rosalinda's fortune-telling salon. I put up a wallpaper trim that shows a woman in Victorian dress entering a gazebo. After the trim was in place, the room was complete. Total cost, sixty-three dollars and fifty-three cents.

There was a couple leaving the room. They were regulars, but this was their first-time experience with the new room. Perhaps they would comment. She was very skinny and wobbled in her high heels walking to his car on the gravel driveway. He wore a fedora and worsted pants, and he always wrote a different name on the card when he registered. Today he was "Ulysses S. Grant." I thought he was a local politician. I was sure I'd seen his picture in the paper, but it was hard to tell with the fedora in the way.

"Interesting room," he said without looking at me.

"Thank you, it's my own design," I responded proudly.

His hand shook slightly as he pushed the key through the half-moon opening in the bulletproof office window. The woman, standing by the car, wrapped her sequined sweater tightly around her small frame, impatient in the cold. He unlocked his side first, got in, and opened her door. In the car, they sat without looking at each other as the motor started. As they pulled away, she smiled and gave me a thumbs-up.

There was another couple waiting in a car. No time to waste basking in my glory, I say. I needed to get Mara to clean the room. She was always sleeping in the linen room. Luckily the intercom was very loud.

"Mara! Room one is done! Hurry, we have a couple waiting!"

No answer.

"*Mara!*"

"I heard you the first time...chill out."

"Don't let Svetlana out. There are a lot of cars coming and going."

"She's asleep on the towels."

I named the cat Svetlana for Stalin's daughter, for whom I also felt great pity. One day the weak, abandoned kitten walked up the driveway and stood in front of the office, and I practically tripped over her when I was leaving. Now the cat was healthy, but she had a bad habit of running across the drive to play with pinecones under the trees. I was afraid she would get run over. Mara always let her out of the linen room when her hands were full with the vacuum and bucket of cleaning supplies.

"Mara—"

"I'm just fixing my hair."

"I forgot to tell you I replaced the vacuum bag."

"How dare you touch my vacuum."

"I made a mess finishing the Gazebo Room. I cleaned up after myself."

"Just kidding, thanks. I'll be out in a minute."

The intercom button got stuck, and I heard Mara say, "Hey, Svetlana, now that she's a big fancy designer I'm surprised she didn't ask me to clean up her mess. Come here, kitty, help me push open the door, my hands are full."

There went Svetlana, right under the pine trees; she was obsessed with those pinecones. At least right now the driveway was quiet. The couple waiting in the car looked anxious. I signaled them to come over.

"How was the room?" I asked Mara.

"The usual—ripped pantyhose, half-drunk bottle of wine, two-dollar tip. They left this."

She handed me a small, thin, square red box.

"What is it?"

"Didn't open it. I was passing by the Roller Coaster Room. The couple in there left the curtain open a crack, and I saw the guy naked standing on top of the bed."

"I'll put it here behind the desk. The customer may come back to claim it. You looked into the room?"

"I couldn't help it. Just as I was walking by, he had his hands in the air like he was on a real roller coaster. Pretty funny." She laughed.

"The fantasy works well. I've already sent the other couple to the Gazebo Room."

"I saw them; they look young."

"It could be their first time."

"I'm going back to the linen room," she said, still half asleep.

"Take Svetlana with you."

"Number two is finished in a half hour."

"Buzz me when you need me."

"I think the intercom is stuck."

"I'll check it," I said.

It was a good thing Mara liked to hang out in the linen room; the office was small, and I preferred to be left alone to study my magazines for room design ideas. I had been looking at travel journals for ideas about a room with a Caribbean theme. I'd call it "Sunset over the Caribbean." There were never pictures of Cuba in these American travel journals even though some of the most beautiful beaches could be found there.

WHUMMMP!

Sounded like something crashed in room two. Svetlana heard it and stopped playing with her precious pinecone. I got Mara on the intercom.

Buzzzz…buzzz…buzzzz…

"*Mara,* did you hear that?"

"Whaaa?"

"It came from room two."

"Let it be, Stalina."

"Sounds as if the television fell off the shelf."

Ring! Ring!

"It's the house phone, Mara."

"Answer it," she said.

"Front desk," I said into the phone.

A high-pitched, excited woman's voice said, "This is room two, the damn Roller Coaster Room. Harry's fallen off your fancy-schmancy bed and hit his head. He's out cold."

"Would you like me to call an ambulance?"

"Are you crazy? No hospitals, no doctors!"

"What would you like me to do?"

"I need some ice to put on the giant egg on his head."

"The ice maker is next to the laundry room. I cannot leave the front desk. I'll have the maid bring you some," I told her.

"We can't go anywhere till Harry wakes up."

"You have a half hour left on the clock."

Her voice deepened into a gravelly smoker's rasp. "He's out cold. It's going to be a while."

"I'll add another hour to your stay."

"Shit, Harry, wake up. OK, what time is it?"

"Three forty-five."

"Harry, what did you do to me?"

"You have until quarter to five. I'll call you at—" I tried to finish, but from the other end all I heard was *click.*

I went back to the intercom.

"Mara, are you there?"

"What happened?"

"The gentleman in room two fell off the bed."

"Is he dead?"

"They need ice; he's unconscious. I gave them another hour."

"I'm not going in there unless she puts some clothes on him."

"Just hand her the ice through the door."

"This job sucks. What was in that box?"

"Get the ice. I did not open it."

"I'll get the ice," Mara said peevishly.

If I didn't push her, she would sleep all day. The red box was sealed on all sides with green tape. Not a very attractive wrapping job. It made no noise when I shook it. I'd wait for Mara; we could open it together. My shift would be over soon, and Mr. Suri would return shortly. I hoped this Harry fellow in room two didn't take a turn for the worse. Svetlana had gone back to playing with her pinecone.

Caww! CAWW!

That noisy crow was always hanging out in the trees. Svetlana was tiny compared to that bird.

Caww! Caww!

The crow didn't frighten Svetlana away with all her yelling. I wondered if the kitten was deaf. Mr. Suri was coming up the drive in his Delta '88. He always took the corner so quickly. The smell of burnt rubber from the tires made me feel warm and happy for his arrival, but I got nervous for the cat because he never watched out for her. I'd get her while I still could.

"Sveta! Svetlana! That's a good kitten. I'll bring a pine-cone into the linen room for you."

Caww! Caww!

"Don't worry, Miss Crow, I won't hurt your kitten. Svetlana, you are light as a bug. No belly yet. Can you hear that noisy crow?"

I thought she heard fine, she just didn't seem to mind the crow's ranting. Svetlana was very scrawny and infested with fleas when I found her. Seeing her reminded me that whenever my mother saw a kitten like that, she would say, "We ate even the skinny ones during the siege."

The Siege of Leningrad was a big part of my childhood.

Chapter Nine: Camp Flora

My city was under siege, and I was sent away. The nine hundred days they cut her off from the world took its toll on my mother.

It was 1941, and Leningrad was having a very warm spring. I was little, only six years old. My parents dressed me in a heavy wool overcoat that was much too big and smelled of mothballs. I threw it off. My mother put it on me again, lifted me in her arms, and looked me straight in the eye. Her breath was warm and smelled of tobacco. She said nothing, but her nose touched mine. Her eyes got wide, and then she shut them tight. I could hear the wooden wheels of the flatbed peddler's carts along the cobblestones downstairs. My father took me from my mother and touched his hand to my face. The high-pitched squeals of the children on the carts came up through our front windows. I wanted to be brave, so I shut my eyes tight to keep from crying. My father put me on his shoulder and walked me downstairs while I heard my mother stand up, knocking over a chair. I opened my eyes and watched as she ran for the toilet in the back hallway. She did not look back at me. As she turned for the door, her dress opened at the back seam. I saw her cotton panties and a teardrop of blood traveling down her thigh. As my father carried me down the stairs, I memorized the pattern of crowns and stars on the blue and white wallpaper in the hallways.

On the street the carts were filled with children, most very young. Many parents were walking alongside the carts. It was chaotic, but somewhere someone was playing a small flute or ocarina. I could not tell where it was coming from, but the sound was a comfort. It went with the rhythm of the carts as they started to move toward the rail station. Everyone looked up, as if the music was coming from the sky. My father placed me in the middle of the cart and pinned one of his poems to my wool coat. I remember the crows flying overhead. *CAW! CAW!* They sound the same everywhere.

"Breathe, Stalina, breathe," he whispered to me. "You're a strong girl; take care of these little ones. When you come home, I will have all my poems waiting for you. You will be my ambassador of words." He hummed a tune in his deep voice as he held my face in his hands, then kissed my forehead before turning to go. I kept the note, and when I was older, I memorized the poem.

My daughter watches the waves by the sea.
Do they remind her without knowing
Of the womb from where she came?
So safe and sound.
Now we are surrounded,
Cut off like the wheat we were meant to grow.
Our bread will never rise or bake.
Will my daughter remember me? When will she return?
Will she have waves of pleasure again,
Or only tears of anger and pain?
Will she remember her place at the table,
And the patterns on the walls?

I leave a thumbprint of a hug around her soft shoulder.
When she returns, will there be anything, anything?
There will be my poems for her.

So many questions in one poem. I would return and commit to memory every one of his poems. The factory whistles sounded for the lunch hour, and the cart moved toward the rail station.

They took us to a camp up north in the region called Karelia, a beautiful area, not far from where my family had its dacha. The children were brought to the town of Kem. We were forty, all from Leningrad. I was one of the oldest. In our camp there were mostly the young ones. The counselors, a mix of students and workers, stayed up all night playing cards in the basement. The smell of vodka and cigarettes came up through the floorboards. The amber light from their lantern streamed through the cracks. I would pass my fingers through the light and make it flicker like an old movie. Moths flying near the lamp would cast giant shadows that looked like hawks circling above our bunks. The buzz from the shuffling cards made the sound effects for the flapping wings of the giant moth hawks I conjured. The slap of a card hitting the table brought me back to reality and to the counselors' daily gossip.

"Lela's parents have not been heard from for a week."

"Don't say anything until you are sure."

"I found a tooth in my soup tonight."

"The children have been working in the kitchen."

"Hazardous work."

"Dangerous eating."

"Balya the cook is missing a front tooth."

"She lost that months ago."

"Maybe I should have saved it for her."

"Gin!"

"Damn!"

"Shut up and deal!"

"Go fuck your mother."

Sounds of scuffling.

"Settle down, Vanya."

"That tooth…I feel ill."

"Buck up. Be glad you're here."

"What, here, at Camp Klorp?" *Klorp* means bedbug.

"Stop it!"

"How about Camp Siege?"

"The young ones will write their parents, 'Dear Uttyets and Mart, Having a lovely time, hope all is well, don't eat Uncle Vanya if you can help it. Your sweet Misha from Camp Siege.'"

"Vanya, please."

"OK, Camp *Flora*, just for you, Tanya. But where's your sense of irony? Not very Russian of you."

Tanya had long blond hair and spent her days chopping wood. She was strong and hugged each one of us every day. It was a comfort. Vanya tended a herd of goats near the camp. He smelled like those goats and had the biggest, roughest hands I have ever seen. I listened while they played cards, keeping very still so that when I fell asleep I would not fall off the bed or disturb my sleep mates during the night. We were always four or more in a bed. When someone near me would start to cry, which happened often, I would try so hard to hold it back. I tried so hard to be strong.

No one escaped the siege. Bela and Leo were brothers who always shared a bunk. Neither one ever said a word.

They ate their meals under the long table and refused to sleep with anyone else. For the rest of us, the bed assignments would change almost every night, so if someone had bony elbows and knees or foul breath, you only had to tolerate them once or twice a week.

"Flexibility, adaptability, and strength—these are the things you will learn at Camp Flora," Tanya told us almost every night before she gave out the bunk assignments.

"Leave Bela and Leo alone," she would say if someone was making fun of them.

One time Rakia, an angry student right out of Herzen University, tried to force them to separate. She was always mad about having to abandon her studies. "It will be good for them," she said in her bossy style.

When they were separated, Leo would not stop hitting his head against the floorboards and Bela obsessively ate the torn threads of a blanket.

"I told you, leave them alone," Tanya said. "I will take care of them."

"But they're not being good Communists," Rakia said, storming out.

"That's not my concern, Rakia. They are children; let them be."

Tanya disappeared one day. Who knows why? In those days it could have been anything. Luckily, Rakia did not take over.

It was two and a half years before I saw my parents again, and at first I did not recognize them or Leningrad. The city was a charred skeleton. My parents were not much better, their faces gaunt and bodies thin as branches. It was my father's smile that brought me back. Even though he had lost a front tooth, I recognized his crooked smile and plump lips. My mother managed a feeble smile through her tears. Neither could pick me up. I was healthy and put my arms around my mother's legs and tried to lift her. She flinched when I touched her. There was great distance between us.

"Stalina, it's not you. My body hurts from being so tired," she said.

Hunger exposes the nerves. Mother bruised easily and was very sensitive to the slightest touch or any sound louder than a light switch. It wasn't until I was older that she told me how they survived.

"We made bread by mixing face powder, sawdust, and tooth powder and fried it all in lipstick for flavor," she explained with her eyes closed.

I was ten years old and asked, "What happened to the stars and crowns wallpaper in our hallways?"

"We stripped it all down and scraped off the glue to make gruel," she continued. "I'd let a ball of it sit on my tongue for a long time."

"How did you swallow it?"

"Imagination. I'd envision the most luscious piece of chocolate cake. I closed my eyes, and when I could smell the cake as if it had just been baked, I quickly swallowed."

"Mmm, let's have some chocolate cake," I once suggested.

"Achh no, it makes me think of eating the wallpaper glue."

My mother's tastes ran to the plain and simple. Soda crackers, boiled chicken, and vodka.

Chapter Ten: Svetlana and the Crow

I had been at the Liberty for more than two years, and Svetlana for almost six months. Each of us was at home here now, perhaps strange to say. The motel was very quiet this afternoon. I got Svetlana and brought her into the office. Mr. Suri liked to play with her.

Caw! Caw!

That crow was very protective of Svetlana. I'd never seen anything like that. She did not fly away when I picked up the cat.

Caw! Caw!

"Svetlana, you are a feisty kitty. Come here. Mr. Suri is back. Let's get back to the office."

As I scooped her up, I saw the remnants of Mr. Suri's drawings in the dirt under the pine trees. He had drawn a map of Windsor Avenue with arrows pointing in several directions and circles around squares that seem to be the other motels. I wondered what sort of plan he was thinking of. The wind had stopped as it often did at this time of day. The trees here reminded me of Lake Ladoga near my family's dacha in Karelia. Pine trees surrounded the water. There was always a bed of fallen needles three or four inches thick that we would walk through to get back to the house. A soft scent of pine followed us as we stirred up the ground in our bare feet. Sticky bits of sap would stick to our toes and heels. I would do a little jig to show off my needle-covered feet, and my parents would clap out the fast rhythms of the *barnya*, a folk dance that builds to an uncontrollable frenzy.

Here at the motel we used a very strong pine disinfectant called King Pine to clean the rooms. It hung heavily in the air and burned the eyes, but ultimately did the job of masking the smells of spilled liquor in the carpets and cigarettes in the drapery. My dream was to scent every room to match its fantasy scene. After all, I was an expert in the arena of aromas. The smell of rain and wet roses for "Gazebo in a Rainstorm" and cotton candy for "Roller Coaster Fun Park." At our lab in Russia, the manufacturing of scents became a cover for the vats of arsenic and anthrax we had in storage for covert operations. Make the poison smell sweet, even if it was an odorless killer like anthrax. I could be arrested for revealing such secrets. Most of the people working in the lab did not know we were making anything poisonous. I knew what was there because the technicians had to come to me for the chemical compositions and the delicate balances needed to stabilize each vat of poison and to create its camouflage bouquet. We mastered over one hundred scents. In addition to the sweet smells of lingonberries and such, we found ways to make the scents of freshly printed newsprint and an electrical storm. Of them all, my favorite was that of freshly baked bread.

"Svetlana, I bet you'd like a room scented with catnip or tuna, wouldn't you, little kitten?"

Mr. Suri came into the office; he looked agitated. There was something about him I found very attractive. It had been a long time since I had felt anything for a man, but he intrigued me. I wanted to know more about him. I liked watching Mr. Suri walk. He had long legs, and his slacks danced around them as he moved. He was graceful, and I thought that he must be a good dancer. I like that in a man.

* * *

"Mr. Suri, how was your day?" I asked, coming in from outside with Svetlana in my arms.

"In order to be approved for a new septic system, it seems I have to join the Kiwanis Club."

"I am familiar with these kinds of things. It was typical in Russia."

"I'm not a joiner," he said. "I just want a decent place for the you-know-what to go."

"Mr. Suri, we have a situation." I attempted to tell him about the comatose customer.

"We will have a very bad situation if I can't properly deal with people's—"

"Yes, well we have a man unconscious in room two."

"Oh great, now the police will come. That's all we need."

"His lady friend didn't want any help."

"He's alive, I hope?"

"I haven't seen him, but all she wanted was ice."

"I could use a drink myself."

I liked how honest he was. "I have vodka," I told him.

"They want me to contribute five hundred dollars to become a member of the local chapter, and then they'll give me the permit to hire another member to dig the leach field that we need to make a proper septic system."

"Leeches?" I asked.

"I wonder how many of the Kiwanis Club brothers are motel customers," he asked. "I'll see at the next meeting I go to."

"That could be very good for business. Five hundred dollars is a small investment," I added.

He played with his mustache. "What about this gentleman in room two?" he asked.

"I added another hour to their stay."

"They have until four forty-five?" he asked.

"Correct. I'll go knock on the door to see how they are doing."

"I don't think you should get involved, Stalina."

"His lady friend sounded upset. I don't mind helping out. "

"It's on your own time," he said sternly.

He put his hand on top of mine. His touch embarrassed and distracted me, and I dropped Svetlana. She scrambled under the desk and was trying to wiggle through a hole in the wall.

"I hope that cat will earn her keep and catch some mice," he said, suddenly placing the hand that touched mine into his slacks pocket, and he jingled some loose coins. I stared at the pocket. The bottle of vodka was in the cabinet under the desk in between a broken fax machine and several rolls of toilet paper. I fumbled around for the cat and at the same time picked up the vodka.

"What's that cat's name again? Vodka?"

"No, Svet-lana," I pronounced her name slowly, "like Stalin's daughter, but Vodka's a good name for a cat. Why leeches?"

"Stalina, didn't you have plumbing in Russia?"

"Leningrad is a very civilized city. There is central plumbing. Sort of."

"And what about in the country?"

"Leeches had nothing to do with it," I said indignantly.

"Some other time I'll explain about leach fields. What about room two? Or excuse me, the 'Roller Coaster Fun Park.' Those rooms might be causing more trouble than we need."

I loved his efficiency, but he worried too much. Little Svetlana would be a good mouse catcher, and the rooms would make him money.

"The kitten needs to go back to the linen room, and then I'll see what's going on in roller coaster land."

"Let her stay here—maybe she'll catch something. Call me if you need anything."

"Thank you, sir."

"Stalina, please stop calling me sir."

"Suri, I meant, Mr. Sur-i."

Outside the wind had picked up again. I'd been monitoring the cracks in the concrete path along the front of the motel. They were getting bigger. The roots from the pine trees were growing under the driveway and breaking up the cement. Mr. Suri's Delta '88 was parked near the trees. He loved that car. It was his symbol of America. My symbol was the Liberty Motel and all it offered its guests. The freedom to love, to share an intimate time away from all your worries. Through my room designs, I had made a place for my customers to let their minds travel beyond their difficult circumstances. They could enjoy happiness, no oppression, for a short time, and it did not cost so much. There was great freedom in the value of my fantasy rooms. They might not be for everyone, but those who came kept returning. I took great pride in this, and it was here I found happiness I had never known. I thought the Liberty Motel was a place of beauty for the soul.

I walked with the vodka bottle in my hand over to the linen room, where Mara was asleep. I hoped she had brought the ice to the Roller Coaster Room couple. The pink door to the linen room stuck like all the other doors.

"Mara," I said as the door whined.

The light was out.

"Mara!"

"Huh," she responded, sounding dazed. "I was having such a bad dream."

"Did you bring the ice to room two?"

"I knocked, but no one came to the door. There was something about a vacuum in my dream. I was outside vacuuming, and one of those crows that lives in the pine trees got sucked into the tube. The vacuum took over and was pulling up everything in sight, including the clouds and the stoplights on Windsor Avenue. I couldn't let go, and the whole time the crow was screeching *CAW! CAW!* from inside the vacuum."

"I think it reflects your conflicts about work."

"Please, don't analyze me. Isn't your shift over?"

"Never mind," I said, closing the door.

"Stalina, what are you going to do with that bottle of vodka?" she said as I closed the door.

"It is to help a difficult situation," I replied.

The door to room two looked like all the others, painted pink with a hammered copper number nailed to the front. I could smell cigarette smoke, menthol mixed with our pine disinfectant. A nice smell, I thought.

Chapter Eleven: Vodka

Knock. Knock.

No answer.

Knock. Knock.

I hear a bit of scuffling.

"Who's there?" a raspy woman's voice asked from behind the door.

"It's the front desk receptionist. We spoke on the phone."

Still from behind the door she said, "I thought someone was going to bring me ice for Harry's head."

"I have the ice."

"Door's unlocked."

The door scraped against the wood frame and concrete entrance as it opened and was tilted to one side like an old person stiff and pitched at an angle by arthritis.

"Hello, I'm Stalina. I thought you might need some assistance."

"I'm Joanie. I don't think Harry is getting up anytime soon. Maybe I should throw a bucket of water on him," she said, leaning on the door.

"How about we get him off the floor? Sometimes if you put the feet up it can help."

"He's too big for me to lift."

She was very thin, and like many women in America she had her hair dyed bleach blond. I myself find black hair has more mystery and drama. Claudette Colbert and Greta Garbo were my role models. Dark and sultry women.

"I can help you."

I put down the ice bucket in which I had placed the vodka.

"Vodka? Good going, I could use a drink. You must be Russian; I like your accent. "

"I thought the situation might call for vodka. It is like smelling salts, and yes, I am Russian."

"I had a Russian boss once. Harry looks pretty peaceful like this, don't you think? He was having such a good time on the bed, or roller coaster, whatever it is. He got carried away, landed on his head."

"I'm glad he was having a good time. The 'bed-coaster' is of my own design."

"I was cheering him on," she said as she touched his forehead with her hand. Her nails were long and painted with elaborate designs. She had dressed Harry in his boxer shorts and an undershirt.

"I gave him these." She waved her hands, indicating the shorts with red hearts. "He likes to wear them when we're together," she said coyly.

"And the shirt?" I asked. It was blue with the word "Waikiki" spelled across it in letters that looked like bamboo.

"His mother got that for him in Honolulu. She used to buy him T-shirts from wherever she went."

"She must love him very much," I added.

"She passed away last year, but Harry was a momma's boy—still is."

Mothers. My mother, Sophia. I'm due to send money to her this week.

"Harry likes to wear nice clothes," Joanie said as she stroked his blue serge suit that hung over a chair. She picked it up and hung it in the closet.

"His suit always smells of menthol cigarettes and spicy cologne, mmm." She buried her head in the sleeve and reached into the pocket to pull out a pack of cigarettes.

I decorated the area outside the closet to look like a game booth at an amusement park. I painted stacks of bottles on the back wall and nailed a lime green snake, a pink pig wearing a tutu, a purple spider, and a monkey with a top hat securely to the wall. At first Mr. Suri thought people might steal the stuffed animals. No one has touched them, and Harry's suit moving in front of the fan looked like someone gearing up and waving his arms—no hands—to throw a ball at the targets.

"Harry once won me a giant panda bear at a fair."

A panda bear is a good idea for an addition to my design.

"Where was the fair?" I asked. "I like to do such things."

"I gave the bear to my niece. About an hour and a half from here in Millerton. No one knows us there. We have to go places where no one will know us."

I had sympathy for her situation. She lit a cigarette. The menthol smoke circled our heads and spread over Harry like a fog.

"Careful with Harry. He's heavy around the middle."

I waved my hands to spread the smoke. "I'll count to three and we'll lift," I told her.

Joanie took off her high heels. The cigarette was dangling from her lips. We counted together.

"One, two, three, lift!"

Harry's weight slowed us down, but with a couple of steps and one final heave we landed him safely on the bed. A moment later one of his legs started to slide off the side. I put my hip against it and pushed his limp body into the middle of the bed. Joanie and I sat next to each other. She stroked his forehead again with her hand. His eyes twitched, and he breathed deeply as she caressed his face.

"Harry's a good guy," Joanie said. "He can be a lot of fun when he's not too stressed out."

The expression was new to me.

"Are there many pressures in his out-stressed life?" I asked.

"I like that, out-stressed. That's putting it mildly," she answered.

"Does he have a great deal of money?" I thought to ask something practical.

"Sort of, but he has two ex-wives and a new wife, who is soon to be another ex-wife. They all cost."

"And you?" I wondered where she fit in.

"I've known Harry forever; we went to high school together. We started spending time together when he was leaving his first wife, Felice. She was a friend. We're all from Hartford."

"So Harry is his real name?"

"It is, but that's not what he wrote on the motel register, is it?"

"No, I think it said Alfred E. Smith."

"Harry's in local politics. He budgets the city's money. Smith is one of his heroes."

"He was a politician in New York. I know, I've been studying for my citizenship. He's the answer to one of the questions. I don't mind waiting with you until Harry wakes up."

"Who is known as New York's 'first citizen'? I bet you that's the question. He studied that guy's life. Maybe we should change his name in the register to Rip Van Winkle."

"I'm not familiar with this political figure."

"Never mind, Stalina. How about a drink?"

I dialed the front desk.

"Front desk." Mr. Suri sounded very efficient.

"Mr. Suri, it's Stalina."

"Yes. What's going on in there?" he replied.

"She needed my help to get him on the bed. He's breathing well. It will be another hour before he comes to consciousness at least."

"They'll owe us for two more hours," he reminded me.

"I know, I'll get the money."

Click.

"Let's have a drink, and then perhaps you can tell me more," I said to Joanie.

Chapter Twelve: More Vodka

Joanie's affection for Harry brought Trofim to mind, and my time with him in Leningrad after I graduated from the Vilnius University. While he was my professor, we spent a lot of time together but never touched. I was in his lab every day; he was a most well-liked professor. While he walked around the lab observing our experiments, he would balance and twirl a beaker on the tip of his finger, never missing a beat to explain where we had gone off on one of our calculations or experiments. When he came close to me, I shivered. Every move he made I felt in my bones; every time he looked at me, I was hypnotized. Trofim was tall and broad; his receding hairline showed off his large head and prominent forehead to great effect. One day I felt his breath on the back of my neck as I labored over the right balance of sulfur, rubidium, and strontium for a plant absorption experiment with a bit of pyrotechnics. I turned my head, and he whispered in my ear.

"Good work, Stalina, you almost have it. Stay after class and I will show you how to finish."

I was so nervous I nearly knocked over my bubbling crucible. When we talked after class, I was so dazed by his attention that I barely heard a word he said about my experiment, but when he asked me to be his assistant I jumped to attention and practically barked, "Yes, sir!" He laughed, told me I had beautiful eyes, and kept chatting.

"What brought you here to Vilnius, so far from Leningrad?"

I collected myself and took a deep breath. "My father went here from 1918 to 1922. He was a writer, a poet."

"I know your father's poetry. He was well respected here. A scholar of great renown."

This was unbelievable to me. I already would have done anything for Trofim; now I was completely under his spell.

"I wanted to know the hallways and classrooms that he loved. It became an obsession," I said innocently.

"You obviously inherited your father's sharp intellect, although I don't know anything about your mother."

"She is also very smart," I said proudly.

He hugged my shoulders with his strong, broad hands and thanked me for agreeing to be his assistant. By the end of the semester, I knew this was more than just a schoolgirl crush when he gifted me with the lab coat and told me he was offered a job in Leningrad.

"I hope we can see each other when I get settled into my new lab at the university."

I had been back in Leningrad for a month when he called. He wanted to see me and show me his lab. He was excited about the work, but lonely in a new city. His family did not join him right away, and even though it was wrong, I could not stay away. I was no longer his student, I was a woman, and as they say, the flesh is weak. And they are right about that. Oh, if it had only been the flesh, it would have been easy to give him up. He made me laugh, he was brilliant, and

I felt inspired when I was with him. He stirred me. No phrase describes it; for once my words cannot express my feelings.

The first time we kissed, spring had finally come to Leningrad after the long, frozen winter of 1954. The ice on the Neva was melting, and snow still held to the ground. The gripping silence of the season was over. Our winters are known for the depths of the cold, but this one was known as "the thaw" because it was the year after Stalin was dead and gone, and everything Soviet was topsy-turvy. Burying Stalin left some with tears of joy to be rid of the monster, while others believed he was our savior. We still had to be careful; you could not trust anyone, so I let my heart take me wherever it wanted to go. I was maybe foolish, but I will never forget my time with Trofim.

The state university set him up with his own lab. His students were hungry for a new era of science and flocked to his lectures. The university buildings are across the river, and from the window of his lab you could see the two-hundred-foot gilded spire of the Admiralty. The river and canals divide the city into many islands. Vasilesky Island is the home of the state university and many important buildings of science. Walking to his lab down the long, long hallway of the school, you could see the beer garden barges and boats filled with tourists traveling up and down the river. The lab was sparse but well equipped. He had changed his research from biology to chemistry and then to physics because it was safest during Stalin's time to be a physicist. Stalin was convinced that in order to build a Soviet atom bomb, they had to employ Einstein's theories. Other sciences and their leading minds were condemned—genetics, Darwin, biology, all denied. The only decoration in the lab was a needlepoint his wife had made having heard about his meagerly equipped lab. It read, "It's better to have a small fish than a big cockroach."

"My wife is very practical," he said.

He stood close enough for our lab coats to touch. I had a sense from the sober look and message of the needlepoint that Trofim was in need of affection. I admired his charts, flickering spectral scopes, and heating crucibles. Out of the deep freezer he pulled a sealed test tube of clear liquid and a beaker that had something purple and gray hanging in frozen liquid.

Jiggling the heavy liquid in the test tube, he said, "This is the best vodka; we make it here from the original recipe of Mendeleev. Let's drink to being together in Leningrad, Stalina."

Mendeleev's chemistry for the distillation of vodka couldn't be outlawed. Stalin could not have Russia without vodka or the atomic bomb.

"What's in the other beaker?" I asked.

"That's my good luck brain," he said.

"Whose brain?" I asked suspiciously.

"T. D. Lysenko, the great scientist and my teacher."

"He was mad. Why would you want his brain?"

"The university thinks I'm doing research on his brain cells. Slicing them and shining a light through the sections to better understand his gifts."

Lysenko's theories served Stalin's desire for the human race to have limitless power over nature. He became the Soviet's ultimate man of science. To disagree meant certain arrest. Trofim played along, and a few years before we met he became part of a team of scientists sent to Siberia to create a race of giant rabbits. The "Rabbit King of Siberia," as his team leader was known, employed Lysenko's fictitious concepts, which claimed an organism could be altered genetically from one generation to the next. The largest rabbits were gathered from all over the Soviet Union to breed. The people were told they would never starve with farms filled with giant bunnies. Trofim's job was to collect the semen from the most oversized specimens. Between this hoax and the wheat Lysenko claimed would grow in the Arctic, millions of our people starved.

"Trofim, don't think me a fool, but that's not his brain," I said.

"Of course it's not, sweet Stalina. I use it to keep my students disciplined. They think I'm crazy because I worship Lysenko, and they never fail to do their work."

He put the flask and beaker down and put his arms on my shoulders. I could see the flickering reflections of the Neva on the yellow ceiling of the lab and in his half glasses. I was fascinated by what filled his fanatical brain. He looked like a sun-lined cloud as he moved over me; his blue eyes were the sky peeking through. His shadow made me shudder with a chill of delight. His lips touched mine, and out of the corner of my eye I could see the fake Lysenko brain warming up in its viscous suspension. If it wasn't Lysenko's, then whose was it? The strong smell of formaldehyde filled the lab. I let my lips go soft, but not too soft, and thought about Amalia's kissing lessons with the plums.

Coming up for air, he said, "I love the smell of formaldehyde."

That was a line from one of my father's more famous poems. On the radio in the lab they were playing Shostakovich's Seventh Symphony.

"You know my father's poem?"

The music reached a thundering kettledrum sequence. Trofim smiled and hummed along with the music.

"My father would play the third movement while he wrote," I added.

Trofim spoke the next line of the poem.

"It preserves the unborn calf with two heads. Will it do the same for my misshapen poem?"

I looked deep into his eyes and could feel the heat on my back as we leaned closer to the lit gas burner.

Then Trofim said, "When we aren't together, it's your lips I think of."

"That's not a line in the poem," I said, amused.

"No, it's not."

His lips had a slight red hue from my lipstick. I loved how his lips were full in the middle and went a bit crooked when he smiled, almost a secret smile just for me.

"Trofim," I said as I took a deep breath, "I think I need a drink."

"Yes, let's make a toast."

Through the test tube, I saw his face, stretched and twisted like in a fun house mirror. He looked beautiful to me.

Chapter Thirteen: Manicured

I retrieved the plastic cellophane-wrapped cups from the bathroom. The photograph of the roller coaster hung over the toilet, I had to say, was a nice touch. I peeked into the shower to check on Mara's cleaning job. Her work was just short of a proper sparkle. You had to get rid of all the residue in order for the chrome to glisten. I had to control myself from pulling out a cleaning rag and finishing the job.

Ring. Ring.

"Stalina, will you answer that?" Joanie said as she sat on the bed combing Harry's thin pate of hair. I picked up the phone.

"Stalina?"

"Yes, Mr. Suri."

"How long do you think they are going to be? I have two couples waiting."

"I'm not sure; we're doing what we can. Business has been good lately."

Click.

"He wanted to know how long we would be," I said to Joanie.

"Harry's sleeping like a baby. Maybe he just had to catch up on some sleep. How about that vodka?"

The "roller-bed-coaster" was designed for physical antics and not necessarily for comfortable sleeping, but Harry seemed very peaceful with his feet raised and slung over the hump. I poured the thickened, cold vodka into the plastic cups. The vapor from the alcohol felt peppery in my throat.

"I hope Harry doesn't wake up; he would have a fit if he saw us drinking out of plastic cups. He says it's disrespectful to the drink," Joanie said as I handed her a cup of vodka.

"*Nostrovya*," I said.

"Here's to Harry, my best friend."

We gulped the vodka down together.

"Harry would like you, Stalina. He likes women who can drink."

"Thank you. There is a Russian saying, 'A drink in time saves nine.'"

Harry made a gurgling sound.

"A drink in time." Joanie laughed. "You Russians."

"Why, is that not the saying?"

"We Americans are just so prissy. We say, 'A stitch in time saves nine.' I love your accent."

"Thank you. I am very proud of my English."

Harry gurgled again and lifted his right arm in the air.

"Maybe he's waking up. Quick, let's have another shot," Joanie suggested.

I went over to get a closer look at Harry. His arm came down with a flop, but it was not only his arm that had risen.

"Look, Joanie, your man is thinking about you."

We both laughed and stared as if watching a newborn's latest discovery.

"That's my boy; he's been having trouble with that lately."

Ring. Ring.

"That trouble seems to be gone," I said as I picked up the phone.

"Stalina, what's going on in there?" Mr. Suri said.

"Mr. Suri, you called only fifteen minutes ago. I think we are making progress."

"I have people waiting. Can we carry him out to his car?"

"Give us a half hour. The hen only eats a grain at a time, but eventually she gets full," I said.

Click.

"What's that?" asked Joanie.

"He's anxious because there are customers waiting for rooms; the motel has become quite popular."

"I like that saying, 'The hen only eats a grain at a time.' I never heard that before."

"Mr. Suri is not a very patient man," I added.

She went over to Harry's blue serge suit and pulled out a large roll of bills from the pocket.

"How much do we owe you for the extra time?"

"Two more hours. That's another thirty-three dollars."

"Here, take a General Ulysses S. Grant."

"Fifty? Ulysses S. Grant was the eighteenth president of the United States."

"Keep the change. You know more about the presidents than I do."

"I have been studying," I said.

Harry gurgled again, and I thought how happy Mr. Suri would be about the extra cash, in spite of his impatience. Joanie and I sat on the floor, watched Harry, and drank another shot of vodka.

"Tell me more about Russia," Joanie said.

"It's still very cold there this time of year," I replied.

"You grew up with all those Communists?" she asked.

"We were all part of a great socialist movement."

"This country dislikes Communists."

"We were friends at one time."

"You guys fought the Germans?"

"The Nazis. They invaded us and we beat them," I said proudly.

"You have such nice nails. Are there beauty parlors in Russia?" she asked, holding and admiring my manicure. She tipped back the remaining vodka in her glass.

"Yes, there are many. I do my own nails; I learned as a child."

Joanie leaned back on her elbows. Harry started to snore.

"We hardly sleep together, so I rarely get to hear him snore. It's kind of cute, don't you think?" Joanie giggled.

"Oolnya's House of Beauty was where I learned about manicures."

"Ool-ya—I love the Russian names, they're so…*vodka!*" she exclaimed.

"Would you like a little more?" I asked.

The bottle of Kremoyna shifted in the ice as if it was trying to get our attention. I just realized then that we'd never used the ice in the bucket for the bump on Harry's head.

"I remember from that movie with Omar Sharif—you drink the vodka frozen even in the winter."

"That is the best way. *Dr. Zhivago*—it was banned for a while in Russia."

"Vodka was banned?"

"The book, not vodka, never, just discouraged, without much effect."

"Let's drink to Ool-ya and her manicures," Joanie said with her glass high above her head. "Maybe Harry needs a sip of vodka."

"It's Oolnya, with an *n*. Put the glass under his nose like smelling salts," I suggested.

"I don't want him to wake up yet. We bought some more time; I want to hear about manicures."

I filled her plastic cup halfway with more vodka and did the same for myself.

"It would be nice to have some herring with this vodka," I said and settled back onto the floor. The room could use a chair or two. Perhaps a bench from a carousel to go with the fun park theme.

"Herring? What about caviar? Isn't that your Russian gold? Fish eggs worth thousands. How strange you Russians are," Joanie said as she went over to Harry and kissed his lips with hers still touched with vodka.

Harry sniffled and turned over, but with a smile on his face.

"Shhh!" Joanie added. "Let's not wake Harry."

"We have another forty-five minutes. Mr. Suri will be calling in a half hour."

"Please, Staliiin-aaa, tell me about Oool-NYaaa."

The vodka had taken effect.

"She called her shop Oolnya's House of Beauty. My friend Olga's mother and my mother would go together for weekly appointments, and we would tag along. Oolnya had massive breasts that were always half exposed, and her behind was so large it made a shelf off the back of her purple satin robe. She sat at the forward edge of her swivel chair because of the size of her behind. She was a bleach blond."

"She sounds fabulous!" Joanie said, enjoying my story and the vodka.

"The banyas all have busy salons. The scent of hairspray mixes with the smell of the saunas and steaming birch leaves right down to the street."

The vapors of the hairspray and acetone took form in the swirling cigarette smoke of Oolnya's clientele. Under those low-hanging clouds, the women made gossip. My friend Olga was destined to be a hairstylist—even at eight years old she could create a hairstyle before touching scissors or curling iron to hair. She also knew everyone's story. It was she who told me that Mrs. Yvashkaya was actually a man, and that the staff at the salon was forbidden to say anything because he was such a loyal customer.

"Oh my. Where is your friend Olga now?"

"She's a legend in St. Petersburg. People come from all over to have her do their hair," I added proudly.

"Hotsy-totsy!" Joanie exclaimed.

"Olga and I would sit under the bubble dryers and read to each other from ladies' magazines and give each other manicures when we were eleven and twelve. She had the most delicate fingers and would paint the polish on every nail with perfectly even strokes. Between the hair dryers going and the piped organ music—this is common in Russian salons—no one could hear us. One time while Oolnya passed by, Olga said, 'Her buttocks are as big as a battleship and softer than the goopiest jar of hair gel.'

"I told Olga, 'I've seen her eating pigs' feet in brine from a jar in between appointments.' Olga told me more details. 'Her lover, Lazlo, sends them every week from the

Ukraine in cases labeled as hair spray so the police won't steal them.'"

"No wonder her ass was the size of Finland. Some men like that, but not my Harry," Joanie said confidently, slapping her bony hip. "He likes to slap this skinny ass of mine."

"Every man is made of different desires."

"And for that I am thankful," Joanie said. "Tell me more."

"Oolnya moved like a hippo with a great sense of rhythm. The top shelves of the supply closet were out of her reach because those hips kept her from passing through the narrow door. When she needed our help, she would say, 'Olga! Stalina! Fetch me a box of cotton balls. I'll give you some for your manicures.'"

"Bossy, wasn't she," Joanie chipped in.

"Everyone who worked at the salon was a bit temperamental. Tasha, the manicurist, was missing the top two joints of her index and ring fingers on her left hand. She had an accident as a teenager climbing over a fence. But the missing joints actually made it easier for her to position her customers' hands and fingers as she did their nails. She was gifted."

"Imagine that," Joanie said.

"When Tasha was in a good humor, she would hand us a bottle of nail polish that was nearly empty. More often she would complain that the salon was the only place women could get away from their duties. 'That includes *children!*' she'd say, making sure we heard. When she chased us away, Olga and I would go into one of the dark, wood-paneled massage rooms in the back to read our pile of magazines and dream about dressing like the models in the pictures."

"Marilyn Monroe was my hero," Joanie added. "Poor thing, it makes me sad to think of her." She got up and walked over to the "bed-coaster" and lay down next to Harry. She had a small pout and a slight quiver on her lips.

"I'm a natural blond, you know," she said as she wiped some spittle from the side of Harry's mouth.

I continued. "Oolnya would rap on the massage room door if someone was scheduled for an appointment. She filled the open doorway completely; her waist made an hourglass shape that we could see around to the front end of the salon. We would get woozy from breathing in hairspray and polish and would stagger off the massage tables and into the salon. Everything seemed to float around us. The peach-colored lace curtains and the kidney-shaped manicure tables became clouds floating by."

"I know what you mean; this room looks all cotton candy soft to me," Joanie said, fueled by the vodka.

"To us, the ladies under the hair dryers with their mud packs looked like an alien race of big brains. One of them once said, 'Looks like those girls have gotten into Oolnya's vodka stash.' Oolnya heard the comment, turned in her swivel chair, lit a cigarette, adjusted her robe, and said, 'I keep only schnapps, to soothe the pain.'"

"I love her!" Joanie exclaimed, and in a terrible Russian accent, she added, "I keep only schnapps, to soothe the pain."

"I like your imitation, Joanie."

"I told you I love your accent."

"How is Harry? Mr. Suri is going to call again."

"Is that the dark man who runs the desk?"

"Mr. Suri? He's not so dark."

"No, he's..."

We both spoke at the same time, with the same words. "Slightly dark."

I added, "He's Indian, from New Delhi."

"Handsome with that mustache, and kind of exotic. I'm mostly German," Joanie added.

"I'm a Jew," I said.

"You're a Jew?"

"You are surprised?"

"You're Russian."

"To the Russians I'm a Jew."

"I don't say I'm a Catholic."

"Are you?"

"Who cares?"

"Why were you surprised?"

"I don't care one way or another. Harry's Jewish. Do you miss Russia?"

"America is not home yet. I do miss Russia."

"That's sad…let's not be sad. More vodka!"

Suddenly Harry sat up with his arms raised in front of him as if he was trying to stop something that was rushing toward him.

"Stop the Shriiiiinnnnerrrs! They're commmminnng!" he screamed.

Joanie jumped toward Harry to keep him from falling off the bed again.

"Harry, wake up!" she shouted as she grabbed him around the waist.

I knocked back the rest of my vodka. Harry was shaking.

"Are you all right?" Joanie was clinging to him.

"I dreamt those damn Shriners were taking over—measly little secretive anti-Semitic toy soldiers. What's she doing here?" Harry said, looking at me. "Owww, my head," he continued, focusing on the bottle of vodka. "Did I drink that?"

"I thought you were over that Shriner thing," Joanie said calmly. "So what if they didn't let you join? Who needs them anyway? This is Stalina."

"How do you do, sir. I'm glad to see you are awake."

Ring.

"Who the fuck is calling me here?" Harry whispered.

"It's OK, Harry, we're safe here," Joanie said, still holding him.

Ring.

"Hello, Mr. Suri." I answered the phone with some authority, and without letting him respond, I continued. "The gentleman is awake, and I will have them vacate in fifteen minutes. Good-bye."

Click.

"Fifteen minutes? What time is it? How long have we been here?" Harry asked Joanie.

Ring. Ring.

"Yes, Mr. Suri."

"Stalina, please don't hang up on me like that. I wanted to tell you that two other rooms have opened up. Everyone is taken care of. Please don't hang up on me."

"Yes, Mr. Suri, I'm sorry. It won't happen again."

"Come to the office when they leave, please. Good-bye."

"Yes sir. Good-bye."

Click.

"He hates it when I call him sir," I said quietly.

Joanie was concerned with Harry, but she still heard me. "Stalina, you like him, don't you?" she said as she started dressing Harry.

Her yellowed eyes looked sad. Her time with Harry was ending for this afternoon. He would go back to his wife, and

Joanie, a bit wobbly from the vodka, would go where? Home? A drinking establishment? Another motel? I stood up. My hips made a long, round arc as I tried to get my balance with my vodka-heavy head. I went over to the stuffed animals and fluffed the purple elephant and adjusted the straw hat worn by the pig in the tutu. The snake stared at me with its googly eyes, and I played with its green felt forked tongue. My animals. My friends. My room. My "Roller Coaster Fun Park." I did not want to leave.

"Mr. Suri is my boss," I said, trying to be sober. "I respect him."

"It's OK for you to like him," Joanie said. "I'm sure he takes your interest in him and his business as a great compliment."

"Do you need help dressing Harry?" I asked.

"I can dress myself, thank you very much," Harry mumbled as he pulled his shirt closed around his paunch.

"I'm glad you're feeling better, Harry," Joanie said, affectionately fixing a misaligned button.

"What time is it? How long have we been here?" he barked.

I answered, "It's five thirty-five."

"Oh shit, I missed my four-thirty," Harry said.

His back was to me as he dressed on the bed. Two patches of sweat were soaking through his shirt on either side of his spine.

"Joanie," he said, going back to whispering, "I've got to get out of here."

"Yes, Harry, how's your head? Here, put your pants on."

I admired him for whispering. He did not want to inflame things, or maybe his head hurt too much to talk loudly. Either way, I was impressed with their relationship. I wanted to ask them why they were not together like a regular couple. They could love each other and take care of each other. The rest of the world would just have to understand. I picked up the bucket of ice and held the cold mass to my chest. The half-melted ice cubes looked like floating skulls swimming around the empty bottle of vodka. I shook the bucket and watched the dance of the diminishing frozen skulls. Joanie looked over at me as she was fixing Harry's tie.

"Stalina, I think we can take it from here. Harry, can you stand up?"

"Of course I can stand. What happened anyway? My head feels like someone took a crowbar and separated my brain from my skull."

"A concussion," I added with concern.

"Not much I can do about that now. You're lucky I can't sue this place."

"Oh Harry, come on. He's obviously feeling better, Stalina. Thank you for everything," she said, winking at me and pointing with her thumb at the bucket with the empty bottle of vodka.

"I was happy to help."

"Look, we really liked the room. Maybe next time we'll take something with a little less imagination." Joanie smiled.

"My newest room is going to be 'Caribbean Sunset,'" I said proudly.

"Save a spot in a beach cabana for us."

"Yes, of course, a cabana," I said as I opened the door and stepped outside.

"Here, Stalina, take the key. I think we're all paid up. I'll take Harry straight to the car."

"Joanie, what are you talking about, cabana?" Harry asked, putting his arm around her shoulder. I noticed then that he was missing the thumb on his right hand. A wound that had healed long ago.

"I'll tell you later, Harry. Let's go," Joanie said as she caressed his damaged hand.

Joanie handed me the key. The nail on her right index finger had broken off, perhaps while she was dressing Harry. He must have had trouble buttoning his shirts with that missing thumb. Joanie saw me notice her broken nail.

"Yeah, it broke. I need a visit to Oolnya's. I liked your story about that place, Stalina. Bye now."

I looked back inside and got a last glimpse of Harry slipping on his alligator shoes. Joanie strapped a gun holster to his ankle. A gun—curious. Why would he need one? Had he ever used it? Was someone after him for wrongdoing? Could it be for revenge or protection? He shook his foot and touched the gun, and then he stood up straight as if the gun gave him the strength to face the world. Someday I might want to hold a gun as well. I could have fixed that broken nail for Joanie, but I hadn't made the offer. Mr. Suri was expecting me.

Chapter Fourteen: Mr. Suri and Me

Walking along the path to the office, I heard the door to the linen room slam shut. Mara would have to come out again soon to clean up after Harry and Joanie.

Caw! Caw!

My cat was under the tree, and the crow was on the ground next to her. She must have escaped from the office. What a strange sight, a crow and a cat together. Svetlana was playing with a pinecone, and the crow was pulling up worms from the ground. I've heard that birds use their sense of smell to locate worms. Like a rubber band, *fwap!* the bird snapped that worm right out of the ground. She shook her head and twisted her neck to get the worm to give up. Maybe she had a nest of chicks and that was why she was so noisy under the trees. She walked over to Svetlana. It was strange how the cat was not bothered by the crow. If she pecked that kitten with her beak, I would throw a stone at her. Gravel. That was all we had here. I'd throw a fistful of gravel from the driveway at her. Wait a minute, Svetlana was opening her mouth—the crow was feeding her the worm. This was impossible. There was a car coming up the drive. The windows in the car were darkened.

"Is there a room available?" a woman wearing a peacock blue shawl asked as she rolled down the window.

"Yes," I replied. "Drive slowly, please. Watch out for my cat under the tree. The office is over there."

"Thanks." As they continued up the hill, I heard her say, "Oh goody, they have a room. I hear this place is awesome, Daddy. Drive slow, watch out for the kitty."

I could not see "Daddy" through the dark windows. Svetlana was still eating from the crow's beak. No one would believe this.

"Sveta, Svetlana, come here to Stalina."

The crow looked at me, said nothing, and flew up to the tree. I crossed the drive and scooped up my bloated kitten.

"Is that lady crow feeding you, little one?"

Svetlana was happily rubbing the sides of her mouth with her ebony and white paws.

"Could it be the crow thinks you are one of hers, my little black cat? The worms are probably healthier than the stuff we feed you."

The foul-smelling cat food we fed her reminded me of the "tourist's lunch," cans of ground fish parts they used to sell in Leningrad in the 1950s when the Baltic Sea had no more fish for the season.

My mother ate the foul-smelling stuff out of some kind of fanatical pride. It was slimy and smelled like a rotten animal carcass. She called it her "fish lover's paté" and always spread it on soda crackers and drank a glass of vodka to wash it down. I was sure they'd used rotten fish and other refuse in the recipe because when you would puncture the can, there would be a hiss and the stench would fill the room. There were times when I was very hungry and would join my mother in this dreadful delicacy. In order to swallow it, I had to first take a sip of vodka, then hold my nose and place a forkful to the back of my throat. Luckily it was ground up like that crow's worm, so no chewing was needed. The museums were being gilded with gold while there was nothing for us to eat. Any tourist who dared to eat a forkful of "tourist's lunch" would have had a true Soviet experience.

* * *

"Svetlana, you would probably love 'tourist's lunch.' You can be sure the cats at the Kremlin were never fed that slop. Let's go see Mr. Suri and ask him what he thinks about your foster mother, Mme Crow."

The wind made the pine trees bend, and the crow kept shrieking at me. I don't think she liked to see me touch Svetlana. Mr. Suri was poring over some paperwork at the desk.

"Good evening, Mr. Suri."

"Stalina, Amalia called. She wants you to call her."

"I saw something very strange out there."

"In room two? What happened? Are they going to sue us?"

"No, they don't want the attention. Something else, under the trees. Svetlana and the crow—"

"What about under the trees?"

"The crow was feeding worms to Svetlana."

"Did you go where I sit?" Mr. Suri asked, somewhat agitated.

"You mean where you draw? Yes, near there. The crow adopted little Svetlana."

"You saw my drawings?"

"The wind blew pine needles over them."

"It sounded like Amalia needed to talk to you."

"I'll call her, but what about the cat and the crow?"

"Maybe we should call a vet to make sure the worms won't poison her."

"I'm happy you have concern for Svetlana."

"I need a good mouser for the motel."

"You hear that, Sveta? You have to earn your keep."

"Let her grow up to be a big cat with a big hunger," Mr. Suri said as he held Svetlana's black face still in his hand for a little moment.

"She's getting a taste for raw meat from the worms. I have a friend who is a vet; let's see what he thinks," he said.

"Thank you, Mr. Suri."

"Stalina, what about the guy who fell off the bed?"

"He got a bit carried away on the 'roller-bed-coaster.'"

"You're sure he's not going to sue us?"

"Absolutely not, and besides, he was fine when they left."

"Call Amalia," he said, handing me the phone. "She's at home."

I dialed. "*Preevyet*, Amalia," I said when she answered.

"*Da...da....da....da...spaseeba. Do svidaniya.*"

I put the phone down slowly and quietly.

"Stalina, is everything all right?" Mr. Suri asked.

"It's my mother; she died yesterday. The rooming house called. They want to know what to do."

"I'm sorry." He put his hand on my shoulder.

"Thank you, she was old and..."

"And what?"

"And sad. She missed the old Russia."

"She missed the Communists?" he asked.

"She believed in our world," I said.

A heavy weight pushed down on my emptied chest. Mother mourned the loss of Russia's collective power. Dementia or not, she knew her world was gone, throwing her into a place filled with fear and anger. It was difficult to catch my breath. A car leaving the motel scrunched and spun in the gravel, and the desk in the office shook slightly from the movement.

"Sit." Mr. Suri pulled up the chair for me. "Is that why she named you Stalina?"

"My name was for protection. Why else would a Jew name her daughter after Stalin? My mother named me Stalina as a joke," I told Mr. Suri.

"What do you mean?"

"She was playing a joke on him."

"On Stalin?"

"He wanted to send all the Jews to Siberia, so she named me after him. His obsession for power was fueled with paranoia. He feared many, not just us Jews. My mother hoped he would never harm his namesake. That's how her mind worked. My mother worshipped and feared him at the same time. My father hated him. I grew up with Stalin's image in my dreams."

"Did you ever meet him?" Mr. Suri was very curious.

"No, not really. Only in my dreams...and my nightmares."

"Did your mother think you would?"

"When I meet someone and they love my name, I know what they believe. In that way it does protect me. Those I can trust hated my name and wanted me to change it."

"But here you are, safe and untouched, so it must have worked," Mr. Suri said. He took my hand.

I could not tell if Mr. Suri was touching me out of pity or affection. I was still having trouble breathing. My mother was no longer breathing.

"I would like to know how she died," I said, staring at a calendar from Domenico's Pharmacy behind the front desk. It was February 16, 1994. She must have died the day before. The calendar's picture of the month was of a pharmacist pouring little oval-shaped blue pills through a paper funnel into a brown jar. On the bottom was an advertisement for a drug called Xanax, with a suggestion: "Come out from under that cloud. Talk to your doctor about Xanax." My eyes started wandering around the calendar. Next to the calendar was a Valentine's Day card from Mr. Suri's son. In Russia there are saints for every day, but the picture of a puppy holding a red heart in his mouth with the words "Be Mine" scrawled across the card made no sense to me. We don't celebrate that day in Russia. We don't need a special day for the heart. Emotions for Russians are like test tubes of boiling sulfurs. Everything is potentially a drama. I noticed that holidays here always coincide with sales in stores. In Russia we have parades.

* * *

"What are those drawings you make?" I asked Mr. Suri. "Are they plans for something?"

"Changes to our little strip of motels. Let's not talk about this now, Stalina. What about your mother?"

The well-fed Svetlana was asleep in my lap. I began to feel sad. It felt like a bony hand was reaching into my gut, twisting my insides, and pulling them down to my feet. A sound was forming in the silence. It was a long, exhausted sigh. It sounded so far away, but it was mine, and it grew into a sob.

"Stalina, I am so sorry about your mother," Mr. Suri said, touching my shoulders. All of a sudden I felt very old. My two and a half years in the USA suddenly seemed very long. My fifty-eight years caught up with me. Death always makes one feel old.

"Tell me something about Russia," Mr. Suri said very gently.

"You should...I mean, you have to give room one a warning." I liked that he was trying to get me to stop crying.

"You are so efficient, Stalina. Soon you'll be running this place."

"Oh no, Mr. Suri, I would never think of..."

Everything embarrassed me—his attention, my mother's death, my feelings—it all made me go slightly faint. I focused on the apple sitting on the counter. Mr. Suri always had an apple for a snack. I began to tell him something from my past.

* * *

"When autumn came, my mother and grandmother closed down our summer house. My job was to take the curtains from the windows and throw mothballs in the corners of the closets and on the beds."

"No wonder you were such a good maid when you first came here," Mr. Suri said, picking up his apple and shining it.

I continued.

"We did not pack up the kitchen. Every pot and pan remained on a hook, all the plates were kept unwrapped in the cupboards, and all the knives sharpened in the drawers. During the last days of summer, there were squash the size of canoes in the garden, and you could not step in there without smashing tomatoes under your feet. Our wooden kitchen table was big enough to seat ten, and in the middle my mother always kept a basket woven by a local farmer from reeds that grew at the edges of the marshes. I used the basket to collect apples for my grandmother Lana's special applesauce. She would say about the big load of the beat-up reds I picked off the ground, 'They may not be very pretty, but I can make delicious sauce with them.'"

"I am a fan of applesauce," Mr. Suri said.

"I would wear the reed basket on my head like a great wizard's hat. The sunlight would filter through the slats and make flickering jewels all over my body. Inside the basket was dark and close and smelled of the earth. We had only four apple trees, but we called them 'the orchard.' The stand of trees made a pool of shade on one side of the yard, with grass underneath that was always cool and moist. I used to lie out under the trees with my dog Pepe, throwing him apples to fetch until his tongue dragged on the ground."

"A dog—maybe we need a dog for the motel? Or here at the front desk for protection," Mr. Suri interjected.

"I feel perfectly safe with the bat under the counter, sir."

"Stalina, remember what I said about calling me sir." He continued to shine his apple.

I went on. "Collecting the apples I'd pretend to be a spy on an espionage mission gathering data on Russia's enemies. One summer, soon after the war was over, we were still unnerved by the Germans. I imagined the apples picked off the ground were battle-weary German soldiers holding secrets and treasures they stole from Russia. The apples picked fresh from the trees were the shiny, bright Americans—our friends who would soon turn and go rotten."

Mr. Suri was rubbing his apple vigorously on his pant leg.

"My grandmother would stand on the back steps, wiping her hands on her apron. I always called her Lana Lana because that was my grandfather's pet name for her. She watched me work under the trees. Proud of her acute eyesight, she'd point to places where I'd missed apples. I carried the basket on top of my head; fifty apples was no problem. She would hold the door open as I ran for the table to drop my load."

"Hold on one moment, Stalina," Mr. Suri interrupted. "I have to give room one a warning."

He dialed the room. "Hello, this is the front desk. You have fifteen minutes left."

"I saw that young couple going in. They looked nervous; I thought maybe it was their first time." I realized that I had stopped crying.

"You should have heard the grunt that came over the phone, Stalina," he said, laughing. "They definitely figured out how to do something with each other."

He smacked his lips with the first bite of the young apple. I continued.

"Lana Lana and I would sit side by side at the table and examine each apple. The bright, smooth ones were for eating, and the nasty fallen ones were for sauce. Separating the apples was our time together. My mother would be at the stove cooking dinner surrounded by the swirling steam from the boiling pots of sautéed onions mixed with rosemary and dill. She looked as if she were floating in the clouds. The rosemary smelled like cedar trees, and the dill had the scent of the ocean. The outside brought inside."

Mr. Suri's mouth was filled with apple as he nodded at me to go on.

"After every apple passed through her hands, my grandmother would select the most perfect one and shine it on her soft apron. She would pull out my grandfather's folding knife. She always had it in her pocket since he died of a heart attack. The knife, opened and glinting, fit perfectly in her broad, well-worn hands."

Mr. Suri had stopped eating and was just listening.

I told him how with the polished apple in her left hand she began the ritual peeling of the fruit's skin in one long spiral. Hoping to learn the subtleties of her moves, I would watch the waxy, red skin drop from the slowly turning apple. She would move the knife through the skin so close to the surface that the white fruit inside remained untouched. At every curve, moving the knife, she would look up to be sure I was watching. The red skin fell like a snake to her feet. It was mine. I retrieved it from between her leather-thonged feet and stretched the shiny peel lengthwise between my hands. Reflections of the kitchen stretched in its slender red curves. She held the apple up to the light. Naked in her hand it was a pearl, the full moon, a finely carved muscle all at once. Sweeter than spun sugar, the smell hit me as I leaned against her big chest and looked up, fascinated by her delicate work. She would then move the knife in her hand and make a slice following the curve of the apple.

"You must always slice the apple before it starts to change color," she explained. Again, with the apple slightly turned, she made another fresh cut, and with a final flip pulled out a perfect wedge, held at the tip of her blade, just for me. "Here, Stalina, the first slice is the best," she would say and watch carefully as I ate the piece of apple.

"I love apples," Mr. Suri said, biting into his again.

"I feel better now," I said.

"What are you going to do about your mother? In India we cremate and send the ashes on a paper boat into the river."

"I think the rooming house can organize a cremation. They are very practical about such things in Russia."

"Will you go?"

"It's very expensive. Olga can…"

"What about Olga?"

"She can help with the arrangements. She has her own beauty salon not far from the rooming house."

"Do you think people need to have their hair done for cremations?" he asked and cocked his head. In that moment I saw him as a very young boy. Innocent and curious.

"No, that wouldn't be very practical. I need to go home, Mr. Suri."

"Home? So you will go? You stopped crying. I'll see if I can get someone to cover your shifts."

"I mean home to Star Lane, not Leningra…I mean Petersburg."

Even though he was being very patient with me, I could tell he was agitated that the couple in the Gazebo Room had not yet vacated. He was staring at the empty room-key hook.

"I can knock on room one when I go to put Svetlana back in the linen room."

"Thank you, I was starting to think I would have to call them again."

He opened the office door, threw his apple core under the pine trees, and said, "That crow eats apples."

I stood up with the sleeping Svetlana in my arms. She barely stirred. When I stepped outside, her eyes opened wide and she stretched her paws.

Caw! Caw!

The crow had flown down to grab the apple core.

"Svetlana, there's your adoptive mother." The cat squirmed in my arms, wanting to get down. "Not now, I'll let you be with her tomorrow."

The couple from room one was coming out of the room as I approached the door. They looked slightly shell-shocked, but they managed to smile as we passed each other.

"I hope you liked the room," I said.

"Very unusual," the young man said.

"Very stimulating," the young girl said with a laugh.

I turned around to watch them and saw her grab the back pocket of his dungarees and hold on to it as they walked to the office. A successful experience in the "Gazebo in a Rainstorm" gives me great satisfaction.

* * *

It was two o'clock in the morning Leningrad time. The same nurse was probably still doing the night shift at the rooming house. She could tell me what happened when my mother died. I wondered if she traded those bras for something worthwhile. I'd only sold one I brought here, but it was very well received. It was the largest one, 85DD, which translates in American sizes to 45DD. A maid who worked for Amalia's cleaning agency bought it. She found it particularly sexy.

She told me, "I usually have to wear bras that look like forklifts. Forget about anything sexy or pretty."

I sold the bra for twenty-five dollars. "What a steal," she said. "Can you get any more?"

I have to say, in Russia we have a great history of lingerie, going back to the czar's French mistresses. There were scandals about frilly undergarments, duels, and champagne while the serfs dug carriages out of muddy ditches.

"Here you go, my kitten Svetlana, back to your linens. Mara, are you here?"

"Geez, can't a girl get a decent nap?" she said, raising her head from between the piles of towels.

"You are going to have to clean the Gazebo Room soon. The couple just left. Your uncle has not called you yet?"

"No, but I expect he'll be sending me a smoke signal soon."

The crackling of the intercom started, and Mr. Suri's voice came over sounding like a soldier reporting from a wartime trench.

"MAR*crrr*A! *crrr*...rooms one...*crr* and four are...*crr* empty!"

"Mr. Suri, it's Stalina. Mara's on her way. Will you call me a cab?"

"*Crrr*...yes, Stalina, *crr*...of course...*crr*."

"Thank you. Someday we'll have a new intercom."

"*Crrrrrrrrr*..."

"Mara..." I started to tell her.

"I'm on my way, comrade."

"My mother died."

"Nothing like dropping a bomb in the linen room, Stalina. I'm so sorry."

"I just found out. I thought you should know."

"I am sorry."

"She was old. I'm going home now."

"To Russia?"

"Star Lane is home now."

Mara quickly gathered her cleaning supplies and was out the door. Svetlana made a sound like a balloon losing air as she circled into a pile of warm sheets.

Chapter Fifteen: Home

The motel signs flapped in the wind as we drove past. The clouds looked like exhausted soldiers marching across a field going dark. The worn tires of the Mike's Taxi Service sedan skidded into the wet curves. To keep from sliding across the plastic seat cover, I held onto a strap dangling behind the driver's seat. With the window open, the rain on my face diluted the salt of my tears. The air tasted like metal. Everything appears to move in slow motion after someone has died—the clouds, the car, and even my tears.

My mother was there, in the corners of the back seat, lingering in the taxi with me. We were often silent together. Standing on a platform waiting for a train, queuing on food lines, or sitting in our apartment watching a shaft of light move across the room. Little or no conversation, just lingering. She was in the shadows somewhere for sure. Even here in Connecticut, USA, I could smell her soft skin and brittle, angel-white hair. Now that she had abandoned her fragile body, ravaged brain, and creaking cot, she was free to roam. Perhaps she had become a rattling cable car on Nevsky Prospekt, or a thornbush in the garden of Anna Akhmatova's house. Maybe she traveled across the sea and entered the cuckoo clock on Amalia's kitchen wall so she could disrupt the silence every half hour. My brain in sorrow and slow motion was a very accepting brain, even for reincarnation. When there is time and no time left at the same moment, we linger, shifting our weight from one foot to the other, our soul seeking a way out. There is a superstition in Russia that when there is a lull in the conversation, another policeman has been born. No wonder there is often discomfort in silence.

When my father died, only the people in Kolyma, the labor camp where he was sent, knew. We received a parcel with his ashes and clothes a year later. It must have taken months in the Siberian cold for his body to decompose. On the shirttail of his prison-issue shirt, almost in tatters, I found something scrawled in charcoal. It was this poem:

Everything here will die.
Never know when, why, or how.
Will the remains remain?
Ashes will float on the air for all to breathe.
The funerals here are defied by our minds.
Never let go. Double-fisted breath.

I transcribed the poem to the back of the photograph I had taken of him when I was young. I stared for days at that photograph, puzzled because I had remembered it differently. I thought he only had one hand on the shovel, but clearly both hands gripped the handle. Every morning I would pull the photograph out from under my pillow where I kept it at night. One day I imagined that his smile had shifted from one side of his mouth to the other. I screamed with surprise, thinking he was still alive in the picture. My mother woke me from the dream and wiped the dust and smudges from my fingerprints on the glass.

45 Star Lane, the taxi will drive...

Just like the last line in the song I made up and sang when I first arrived here two years ago. *Moscow, Kennedy, Port Authori-tay!* That adventure felt like ancient history. But there I was, again being driven to 45 Star Lane. I really could use a song now, I thought. I'd add something to this old one, like letting out a skirt when your waist has gotten too big. Just another line or two would do. 45 Star Lane is quaint on the outside and shoddy on the inside. When I first came here, it looked like a fairyland of perfect little houses with birds singing on wires and the wind rustling from the tops of the trees down to the blades of grass on the square lawns. Behind all this, the houses had walls so thin that from any room in the house you could hear someone turning the pages of a magazine while they sat in the bathroom. The windows didn't keep out the wind and the rain, so the sills had gone rotten from never drying out. Lately I'd noticed a mold growing where the windows met the walls. I'd been spraying disinfectant, the same we used at the Liberty Motel, to try to kill the spores, but it had done nothing. Chain-link fences divided the houses into scraggly lawns that were decorated with painted wooden cutouts of plentiful women's behinds rising into the air. The make-believe gardeners were bent over tending to their pansies and impatiens. Bulging roots of the sycamore trees had come through the sidewalks like arms and legs of waking giants. The neighbors kept to themselves.

45 Star Lane, the taxi will drive,
A quaint white house with rotting windowsills.

Amalia might not appreciate this new line. I could add something more pleasant.

I live with Amalia, and we both pay the bills.

The taxi arrived at my home.

"Thank you, sir, you are an excellent driver."

"Mike's Taxis, you can always count on us, miss."

When he turned around, I could see that his handlebar mustache had crumbs stuck in the sides and he was wearing a cap with a picture of a fish.

"Do you like fish?" I asked.

"Bass season starts soon. How'd you know?"

I pointed to his hat.

"My girls sent me a year of *Bassmaster* magazine for my birthday."

"They must appreciate their father very much."

"Nah, they just like to get me out of the house."

The radio started to squawk. He picked up the mouthpiece. "Bassman, over."

A woman's voice came on. "Hey, good lookin', get that junk heap of yours over to Charleston's Bar. Barry needs a ride home; his wife has to leave for work. Over."

"That's Randi; she's a ball buster," he said, looking at me in the rearview mirror.

Then into the radio again he said, "Keep your titties straight, mama, I'm on my way. Over."

"Fuck off, lover, over," she replied.

"I'm just finishing up with Star Lane, sweet meat, over."

Then he turned back to me. "She and I have known each other since high school."

"I live here with Amalia; we've know each other since we were children."

"Are you going to be all right?" My swollen eyes must have concerned him.

"Yes, thank you, now that I am here. It's my mother; I just found out she died. She was still in Russia."

"I'm sorry. It's like that, people and things go away, they end, leave us to ourselves."

"Yes, they do. Thank you, Mr. Bassman."

I was still holding on to the strap behind the driver. It was a comfort to hang on to something. I drifted back to St. Petersburg for a moment as I started getting myself out of the cab.

* * *

"It's just not practical. We are not going anywhere," Trofim had said without looking in my eyes.

It was a summer night. I was just nineteen and in love.

We met to watch the bridges go up over the Neva.

"Opening the bridges *is* a practical thing," I said. "We may not be able to travel to the other side of the river, but it saves the government money. They don't have to pay anyone to operate the bridges through the night."

He wanted to end our relationship, not debate bridge operations.

"Stalina, this is not about the bridges," he said, looking down at the water.

The river was black and oily. Our faces reflected in the lapping waves looked like photographs developing in a darkroom. I watched the light in the sky disappear. It was gone for just minutes, and when it began to get light again, Trofim was already walking across the bridge before it was even fully down. He never turned around. I stood motionless until everyone rushing to get home to change for work pushed me along the canal. He was gone. It felt like someone had died.

* * *

Many years later, in Connecticut, USA, I felt a similar emptiness. As I stood outside the cab, the rain started coming down harder. My cheeks stung with the salt of my tears. I leaned through the window to pay the driver.

"It's been taken care of, miss. Your boss paid for the ride. Go. Get out of the rain." He shook the crumbs from his mustache.

"Mr. Suri is a very nice man," I told the driver.

I heard the dispatcher's voice over his radio again. "Move it along, Barry the Barfly just fell off his barstool."

"On my way, general, ma'am," he said to the radio. And then to me he said, "Take it easy, miss. Get yourself inside." He drove away.

Amalia opened the door and came out with an umbrella over her head. "Stalina," she said, "come in out of the rain. You're home."

It was good to be home.

Chapter Sixteen: Invention

I wondered if the people at the rooming house mourned for my mother, if anyone was there when she died. I'd have liked to know how it was for her. I felt badly that I had not stayed until she died.

"Stalina, I've made some tea. Come sit," Amalia said as she guided me to the kitchen with her arm around my shoulder.

"It's too early to call St. Petersburg," I said, looking at the cuckoo clock.

Eight hours' difference. Seven thirty here, three thirty in the morning there. Time changes, but the distance stays the same.

"It will be morning soon. You'll be able to call in a few hours," Amalia said quietly. "I'll sit with you."

"Thank you, that's very kind."

"Stalina, I was sorry to have to tell you about your mother."

"When I left, she was angry and sad and sick. I wanted her to come with me."

"She wanted to die in her Leningrad," Amalia reminded me.

"Yes, probably so. She never did like calling it St. Petersburg."

"It was her choice. Will you go?"

"The nurses at the rooming house can make the arrangements. Do you think I need to identify her, or sign for her in person?" Suddenly I wasn't sure.

"I wouldn't know, but it has to happen soon. They aren't going to keep her around."

"I could barely get there in time for everything to happen as it is supposed to."

"Speak to the nurses first, then we'll see," Amalia said. Pulling a small package out of her purse, she continued. "Let me show you my new glass figurine. It's a terrier; it reminded me of your dog when we were growing up."

"Pepe?"

"I couldn't remember his name. Doesn't this look like him?" she said as she pushed the glass figure across the kitchen table to show me. She collects glass miniatures that she displays on the windowsill in the kitchen. A unicorn, a turtle, an elephant, and a replica of the Cathedral of the Spilled Blood from home.

"I loved that dog."

"What happened to him?"

"My father had him put down. It was that little wretch Nadia's fault."

"I don't remember the details, Stalina."

If Amalia wanted to distract me from my sorrow, she was doing a good job. When Pepe was taken away, at first I was very sad, and then I was angry.

"Tell me about Pepe," Amalia insisted.

I explained how after months of tears and temper tantrums, my parents allowed me to have a dog. As an only child, I longed for a companion. My friend Mina had a canary, and my parents thought a bird was a good idea for a pet. I told them the cage bothered me, and when I visited Mina, it was all I could do to keep myself from letting the poor bird go free.

Pepe came from the cages of a dog pound in Leningrad. All those dogs waiting and barking—I wanted them all. The moment he was let out of the cage, he stayed by my side. He was a full-grown terrier mix and seemed very relieved when I fastened the brand-new red leather collar around his curly brown neck. He loved to dig in our backyard and bury things in the crumbly black soil.

On a warm Sunday in August 1949, Mikhail and Andrei, the twin brothers with identical limps who lived next door, and Nadia and Lara, the two blond-haired sisters, twelve and nine years old, whose backyard faced ours, came over to play. The adults were playing cards and drinking tea in the shade. Nadia immediately began organizing and explaining the rules to the game that would alternately put one of us in the center of a circle reaching to catch a fist-sized beanbag tossed overhead. If you caught the bean-bag, you got to choose someone to kiss behind the old cherry tree.

"We all stay seated," Nadia explained. "That's what makes it hard."

Pepe was running around our circle wanting desperately to take part, but Nadia would not let him.

"Why don't you tie that unruly mongrel up? He's ruining everything," she said, just like an adult.

"Don't be such a big boss, Nadia. He will sit when I ask him to. Here boy, Pepe, Pepe," I said. He was panting, looking longingly at Nadia's left hand, which held the peach-sized beanbag with a tight, controlling fist.

"Pepe is spirited," I told Nadia, trying to smooth over his bad behavior. He'd pull on his leash every time he'd see a pigeon on our walks, and he barked loudly at anyone in a uniform. My mother once had words with the traffic police when Pepe was in the car, and from then on, he became protective and upset whenever a uniform approached any of us. You can imagine in the Soviet Union, this made for a rather stressful existence.

In the backyard, on that afternoon, he was just having a good time, feeling like a puppy again, chasing around our circle, stretching out his front paws, ready to jump and pounce in any direction.

"Pepe, sit! Sit! Good boy," I told him.

He could not be contained that day. When Nadia finished explaining the rules, she too sat in the circle. Pepe ran to her side, still panting over the beanbag. She twisted her body toward Pepe, confident that she had the power to control him.

"Sit, you sweet mutt," she said. "Now lie down, lie down."

Sitting was all Pepe could handle, but Nadia began pushing his head down toward the grass.

"Lie down." She pushed again. "Lie—"

Her forceful hands and controlling spirit brought out something ugly in Pepe. He snapped and lunged at her. It was a motion of protection, but his sharp side teeth caught the fleshy part of her soft, pale, fourteen-year-old jaw. I watched as the blood spurted through her shaking fingers.

Amalia had heard only rumors about this story. When I finished telling her about this last part, she stopped me.

"Stalina, the story I heard was that Nadia smacked Pepe because he was misbehaving, and that you tried to bite Nadia, but Pepe got to her before you did."

"Rumors. I wonder what they would have done to me if I did bite Nadia. She certainly deserved whatever she got."

Amalia added, "She never wanted to play with me."

"She was jealous that you got to wear makeup," I assured her.

"She thought I was a horror with this mark on my face. She couldn't stand to look at me."

"Spoiled brat."

"Did the bite leave a scar?"

"Plastic surgery. There was only the slightest line along her jaw."

"What about Pepe?"

"The rest of that day was like a bad dream." I continued the story, and Amalia made more tea.

"Nadia rolled on the ground holding her face with her hands. The blood seeping through her fingers looked like worms slithering into the ground. The grass moved beneath my feet; my voice was gone. The adults ran in all directions like a bomb had gone off. I stood in the middle of the lawn, fixated on Nadia. The twins, Mikhail and Andrei, chased after their parents as they ran next door to call an ambulance. Pepe was cowering under the pine trees at the edge of our yard. I could see he was sorry and scared for what he had done."

"The poor dog," Amalia said as she poured the hot water over the tea.

"My father screamed at me, 'Stay away, he's gone mad!'"

I told Amalia how my father rolled a newspaper and grabbed one end like a club. My grandmother held Nadia's bawling sister in her arms and started singing to calm her down as she brought her inside. The emergency medicals came and took Nadia away. I followed my father as he walked silently toward Pepe. The dog's eyes were deep, dark pools of fear.

"I wanted to comfort Pepe, hold him in my arms and let him know I understood it was not his fault. The rage in my father's arched back frightened me. I watched his biceps engage as he raised the paper like a thug with a nightstick. I still could not speak, but my brain screamed at my father's unflinching raised hand. 'Don't hit him. He'll never do it again, I promise!'

"When his arm came down, the newspaper made a hard crack against Pepe's spine. The poor dog made no sound but crawled further under the pine trees. With his back swayed, he looked up at my father's raised arm, waiting for it to fall again. It was my father who had gone mad. Rage and pain had overtaken him."

"Powerless," Amalia said as she stirred her milky tea, "as children we were powerless."

"Helpless, I felt so helpless. My mother grabbed my father's arm, and he looked at her strangely. I thought he might hit her, but he stopped."

I remembered how the tightly rolled pages of *Pravda* loosened from his hand and rolled along the ground. Pepe crawled to the coolness and shade of the apple trees. My parents stood together, their heads lowered.

"Have a sip of tea," Amalia said, pushing the cup and saucer closer to me.

I continued, "Hearing my grandmother and Lara laughing in the kitchen brought me out of my state of paralysis. They were slapping and kneading the bread Lana Lana had left in the cupboard to rise earlier in the day. I felt invisible. No one saw me going to Pepe. I stood over him; he growled and bared his teeth pathetically. My voice came back. 'It's all right, boy. I'm not going to hurt you.' I spoke until his body relaxed. I touched his soft pink ears and caressed his furry chin. He liked being tickled there, and he closed his eyes with relief."

"What happened after that?" Amalia asked.

"That night Pepe was locked in the basement and was not allowed to sleep in my room. After everyone was asleep, I took my pillow and sat by the basement door. I could hear Pepe's panting, and I told him, 'We'll go to the beach tomorrow for a run. You'll swim in the river, and we'll walk together, like always.' I fell asleep at the door. When I woke in the morning, I was in my bed. In the kitchen my father was reading the paper, and my mother was making yogurt. The door to the basement was open, and Pepe was gone. I asked about his whereabouts.

"My mother said, 'A farmer took him to chase the rats out of his barn. He'll be happier there.'

"I was met with silence when I asked if I could go visit him. Later that evening I found his collar in my mother's dresser when she sent me to fetch her sweater. I left the collar where I found it. The next day I went to look at it again, but it was gone. Neither my mother nor father ever said anything about Pepe again. Soon after that my father was also gone."

"Well, now that we've heard that nice cheery story, Stalina, what about your mother?" Amalia's sarcasm was amusing even during this difficult time.

"Cremation," I said matter-of-factly. "I'll arrange to have her cremated. The rooming house must have a place they store ashes until relatives can pick them up."

"Ashes A to Z."

"Ashes to zashes. Interesting sort of library."

* * *

I waited until it was six in the morning to call the rooming house. The same nurse I gave the bras to before leaving was on duty. She would make the arrangements for the cremation, and she informed me that they could only hold on to the ashes for a month. I told the nurse I would send her two hundred American dollars and that my friend Olga would retrieve the ashes and collect the picture of my father and the locket of Lenin my mother always wore.

Amalia went to the sink and splashed some water on her face before making a pot of coffee. My tea, made minutes before, had gone cold.

She sat next to me and reached for my hands. Her hands were still wet, and the cold made the hairs on my arms stand up. Lifting my hands in the air, she said, "Come on, Stalina, let's dance for your mother."

She sang.

Happiness for all,
On this earthly ball!
Happiness for us,
Before we take that final bus!

We sang together.

Bus!
Bus!

Bus!

We danced around the kitchen and banged pots and pans, making a racket. Amalia's son, Alexi, came up from the basement and gave us a disapproving look as he opened the refrigerator and took out a container of milk and some leftover chicken. He had become very handsome in the last two years. He was sixteen and had let his dark brown hair grow to his shoulders and parted it in the middle. Around his neck he wore a thin piece of leather as a choker with a small skull in the center over his bulging Adam's apple.

"Stalina's mother has passed away," Amalia told him.

He took a bite and said, "Sorry to hear that. It sounded like you were celebrating."

He went back downstairs with a chicken leg in his mouth, the carton of milk, and a box of gingersnap cookies under his arm. I could hear music with a loud bass beat coming from his underground lair.

"Alexi stays up all night and loves to snack in the morning on leftovers. His father was exactly the same," Amalia said as she sat down and put her head in her hands.

Her husband, Yossef, was a construction worker who died when he fell from the roof of St. Isaac's Cathedral. He had been part of a crew that was repairing the copper gutters. Alexi was only two years old then. Yossef's death was considered his own fault because the police found a half bottle of vodka under the seat of his car. Amalia and Alexi were isolated and scorned because Yossef's actions were considered a crime against the state. Amalia made a public appeal to clear her husband's name. She told the authorities it was her bottle of vodka and that he only drank beer because it helped to steady his hand. If it had been beer, he would have been a hero, but giving a bad name to vodka was a no-no. The authorities believed Amalia's story, but they were still unhappy with the mess Yossef's splattered body left on the plaza outside the cathedral. A couple who were sitting on a bench kissing when the accident occurred filed for trauma assistance and were given two months' pay and an apartment in the country to go to on weekends. Amalia received nothing. She left Leningrad angry and sad. That was 1980.

The cuckoo clock struck half past six; the sun was just starting to come up. It was otherwise very quiet in the kitchen. Amalia's cats, Shosta and Kovich, wandered in for their morning meal. Amalia dried her tears with the palms of her hands and kissed my forehead before going off to bed.

"Thank you," I said.

"You look tired, Stalina. Why don't you go to bed, too," she said as she held my face between her hands.

"I will, after a while."

I went outside and sat on the front stoop as the sunlight began to spread across the patches of grass and mounds of dirt and rocks in the front yard. Amalia had started to dig things up to put in a garden. The ground was very hard, so she had worked it with a pickax and a shovel. She left her shovel standing upright, wedged between two boulders. It reminded me of my father's shovel in the photograph I had taken so many years before, and one of the many poems he wrote about gardening tools. Working in the garden inspired him. The morning light came through the trees and warmed the handle of Amalia's shovel. One of Father's poems was about Mother and her garden. He called it "Sophia's Garden."

My wife stands by
With our shovel in her hands,
Another cedar, birch, juniper, or
Wisteria to address.

A woodcut from the thirteenth century
Shows Deucalion, son of Prometheus,
Shouldering a mattock.
Agrarians one and all,
His wife, Pyrra, stands by with a long-handled shovel,
Fields and beds to cultivate.
Having escaped the efforts of Zeus to destroy all mankind,
They survived his viral floods,
The waves receded,
At Parnassus, they rebuild on higher ground.

My wife stands by and
I take the shovel from her soft hands
To dig a ditch, move some stones,
Feed our family,
Cultivate.

From Roman forge to smelter's hammer,
Revolution of industry,
The shovel,
Ancient, knowing tool,
Invention that can serve us all.

My wife stands by,
Holding in her arms the iris, peonies, and daylilies,

Listening for the sound
Of the shovel digging deep into the earth.

Like the deity survivors before us,
We stand with hatch, hoe, trowel, scythe, and sickle,
Our tools taken back from the hands of thieves,
Our bodies smeared with blood,
Washed away by the rains of time.

My wife stands by,
Her arms open wide.
She shows off her gladiolas, lupines,
And bleeding heart vines.
A shovel,
And the sun to shine,
Is all we need for now.

Chapter Seventeen: Commuters' Dream

The sun was up and Amalia was sleeping after staying up so late to grieve—and dance—with me after my mother's death. I could hear her wheezing from down in the kitchen. I wouldn't disturb her by going up the creaky stairs to my attic room. I'd go back to the motel. It was six forty-five in the morning. Mr. Suri would be tired but happy. It was most likely a busy night. Business picks up when it rains.

The people riding the bus at this hour, only seven in total, were mostly women who took care of the children and houses of people who went off to work in Hartford city center. We rode the bus as one that morning. All our energies propelled us through the streets of Berlin, Connecticut, to our places of employ. We were the workers of this dying city. It *is* dying; otherwise there would not be an underworld in which the Liberty Motel and the other short-stay establishments could survive.

My clothes were still damp from the rain of the night before. The sun was coming through the trees, but the massive dark clouds were moving overhead, and the wind had gone sharp and cold. The bus passed the same places I saw when I first moved here. Who could ever forget Pete's-A-Place or the Glass Eye Emporium, which appeared to have closed its doors for good. The sign of a human eye with a blue neon iris was outside the store in a heap of discarded wooden cabinets, small round mirrors, and metal chairs with headrests. I wondered where their customers go now.

The road was slick and shiny, and the smell of rain and oil seeped into the bus as the wheels spun along. The woman sitting across from me was wearing a white uniform that was much too tight for her. Her ankles were swollen in light-colored panty hose, and she was knitting an infant-sized sock on three small needles out of multicolored yarn. Next to her was a young woman, with thin arms and long hands, who was sleeping with her head tilted slightly to the left. She reminded me of one of the cranes that nested in the grasses along the shores of the Gulf of Finland. The woman next to me still smelled fresh from her morning bath. The scent of peaches surrounded her. She had a large book open in her lap. I could see it was a textbook for nursing. She was reading about techniques for drawing blood.

"Ask the patient if they are right or left handed. Wrap the rubber tourniquet around the upper arm of the hand they use less frequently. Tap with two fingers on the top side of the elbow joint," the instructions explained.

A shadow cast from the sun coming over our shoulders looked like a bird landing across the page where needle insertion was described. As I leaned my head back and looked up and out the window, I could see a cloud in the shape of a dog's head. Its mouth was wide open, and it looked like the dog was howling at the fading moon. The seats in the bus were molded blue plastic, and the dry heat came up from behind my legs. My clothes had dried and no longer stuck to me. The bus driver was wearing a black kerchief tied around his head. He was sweating quite a lot and kept pulling out a bandana every few minutes to wipe his forehead and neck. The other seven people on the bus were silently staring into the middle aisle as if it were a bottomless canyon. My eyes felt tired and swollen from the crying and lack of sleep. I wondered if my sadness made me smell different. The woman with the book closed her eyes and started to sleep and lean against me. She must have been tired from working and studying and going to school. The book was slipping off her lap.

"Here, miss, your book." I grabbed it before it fell to the floor.

She woke and said, "Oh, I must have fallen asleep. Thank you. I am very tired."

"You are studying?"

"For nursing. It's very hard."

"You smell like peaches," I said, hoping to make her feel more comfortable.

As I handed her back her book, she said, "Thank you, it's my shower gel."

"In Russia everyone goes to the local banyas. We love special smells, especially of flowers and fruit trees."

"Banyas?"

Her straight brown hair was pulled back tightly in a ponytail, which exposed her high forehead. She was young but already had some fine lines surrounding the edges of her blue eyes.

"A bathhouse," I told her.

"Men and women together?"

"No, separate. We use birch branches to take off the dead skin. It awakens the circulation and stimulates the spirits."

"I use a loofah, and sometimes that's a bit too rough."

"I miss the banyas. Too bad there isn't one here in Berlin."

"Bathing with a bunch of other women—I don't know if that would be considered a good time here. This is my stop, excuse me," she said as she got up to stand by the back door.

"There is no other way to get as clean. In the heat and steam of the banya, you can feel your skin as a living, breathing part of you."

"Whatever floats your boat," she said as the door was about to open.

"*Do svidaniya*," I said.

In Petersburg at the metro stop closest to my local banya, there was always a group of women singing in the tunnel during the busy commuting hours. People would toss money into a hat they placed by their feet. One of the women was well dressed; she probably worked in an office. Another was much older and walked with a cane. The third always wore a hodgepodge of ethnic clothing: a babushka scarf, an embroidered peasant shirt, and a batik wraparound skirt. She was the great harmonizer. Their voices resonated off the curved ceramic walls of the tunnel and made a river of sound flow under the canal. Strong, steady, and deep, the music was a caress when you walked by. When they had collected enough money, they would pack up and come to the banya for a steam and glasses of vodka. They would beat each other with the birch branches in the same rhythm as the folk songs in their repertoire. Everyone's skin glistened from the repeated swipes with the softened branches foaming with eucalyptus soap. Every pore was stimulated. People here would benefit from such camaraderie and cleansing.

The bus driver kept wiping his brow. He looked agitated. Thinking about the banya soothed me, and I closed my eyes as a patch of sun coming through the clouds blinded me for a second or two. In the darkness I escaped this painful morning with a fitful dream.

* * *

"Garghhh...garghh..."

Strange noises from the bus driver.

"Excuse me sir, are you all right?" I asked.

His right arm had dropped to his side.

"Garghhh...garhh..."

He couldn't speak; he was choking. He was turning around to look at me.

The bus was still moving. Everything else shifted to slow motion.

I saw the nursing student waiting at the rear door, and I saw myself sleeping. Suddenly, the driver slumped over the wheel, and jarred out of our early morning stupor, we all started clamoring over each other. Things started sliding and tipping over as the bus skidded. The world outside the bus streaked by as it spun and slid. The mist rising from the road turned into a belt of clouds around the bus. I saw the nursing student jump past me to the front of the bus. Suddenly everything stopped and there was silence. The rain had started to come down heavily again. I was on my hands and knees. The woman in the white uniform with the swollen ankles was clutching her knitting. The nursing student was under the feet of the driver holding down the brake.

"Are you all right?" I asked.

"I think he's dead," she said.

We were all silent for a moment, and then the woman with the knitting started softly crying. Luckily, it was still early and the roads were not busy, but in just a few seconds, several cars coming in either direction stopped just short of hitting the bus. People came out of their cars and gathered around it.

"I'm afraid to take my hand off the brake," said the nursing student.

There were beads of sweat on her upper lip. I approached her slowly. It was as if the bus was dangling off the edge of a cliff. The key to the ignition was on the floor just below the driver's dropped hand.

"He's dead," I said.

The nurse and I stared at the key.

"Do you think he shut the bus off before he died?" she whispered.

"He must have been very well trained," I added.

"The emergency brake, can you reach it?" she asked.

I leaned over the driver and pulled the lever on the brake.

* * *

I woke as the brakes screeched as we stopped for a red light. Startled out of my nightmare, I hit the window with the back of my head. The bus driver was just fine and steering his vehicle straight ahead. My fellow passengers were as they had been, sitting, staring, knitting, and sleeping. The next stop was mine.

The arch-shaped neon sign for the Liberty Motel glowed like a radon tube in a frozen centrifugal chamber, just like we had at the old lab. In the morning mist the motel looked otherworldly, like a good setting for a mystery. If I'd let my fantasy continue, the police and several ambulances would be arriving at the scene—a good opening for a gangster story. As the accident occurred, simultaneously a dark car would be disappearing through the mist up the motel's driveway. Then the scene would shift to the inside of the bus. The nursing student would have the first line. "Is anyone hurt?" she would say. The other people on the bus would brush off, stand up, and start gathering their things from all over the bus. We would hear various comments from the passengers.

"I think I'm OK."

"I lost my purse."

"Where are we?"

"I can't find my shoe."

"I dropped a stitch."

The character playing me would have bumped her head and suffered amnesia. She would not remember that her mother had died or why she was on the bus. A police officer with a crowbar would pry open the door of the bus. There would be a rush of activity, and the emergency medicals would pull the bus driver from his seat and lay him down to resuscitate him. They would pump his chest and throw an oxygen mask over his face.

"I need to get to my job at 27 Blodgett Hill Road," the woman with the knitting would say.

The pumping and pushing on the driver would make it look as if some life was coming back to him. But when they stopped working on him, there would be only silence. My character would get off the bus, dazed from the event, and start to wander up the hill, mysteriously drawn to the motel.

Her boss would be coming down the hill to see what all the commotion was about. Upon seeing her, he would run to greet her, and she would fall into his arms, not knowing who he was or why he had embraced her.

My fantasies run deep.

* * *

The doors of the bus opened. The bus driver was still wiping his brow.

"Thank you, sir," I said.

"Have a good day, ma'am," he replied.

The scent of the pine trees on the sides of the driveway leading up to the motel mixed with the strong smell of bleach from the laundry room and made it feel as if I were walking through a sterilized forest. My eyes watered and the tears burned as they streamed down my face. These were chemically induced tears. They were not salty like the tears for my mother.

As I walked up the hill to the motel, there was no greeting from my boss, just like there was no accident. The light was still on outside the office. I could hear the rumble of the washing machines; Mr. Suri must have put in a load of linens. There were several black cars lined up in the parking lot. The motel was busy for such an early hour.

The next bit of my story will explain how my life in Berlin, Connecticut, and in the world, suddenly and completely changed.

Chapter Eighteen: Mr. Suri and the Mob

Apparently, Mr. Suri had a bad reputation that I was not aware of. When I walked into the office, he was not alone.

"Stalina, what are you doing here so early? This is not a very good time," he said.

He was seated in the office chair, several men in dark suits wearing mirrored sunglasses surrounding him. The office was close and steamy from all the bodies. They were like a pod of seals jockeying for space on a sunny piece of rock. Any one of us was about to jump or get pushed off.

"I couldn't sleep, and I had nowhere else to go," I told Mr. Suri.

"Who is this dame?" one of the black suits asked.

"She just works here. She doesn't know anything," Mr. Suri explained.

"Stalina, what kind of a name is that?" the same suit asked.

"I'm Russian," I said. "Ever heard of Joseph Stalin?"

"Stalina, don't be rude to these gentleman," Mr. Suri warned.

I understood the irony from his tone. These were not gentlemen, but small-time hoods acting like big-time gangsters. I cared for Mr. Suri and could tell he was in a prickly situation. It was a mystery to me that would soon be revealed. I understood this to be a delicate circumstance, and I would, as they say, play my cards right.

"Hey, the boss is Russian. Maybe you know her; Nadia Tamovsky is her name," said the short, squat black suit with a widow's peak and a pencil-thin mustache.

"The *N* is for Nadia? I thought your boss was a he. You always just called her Big N," Mr. Suri added with surprise. "You work for a woman?"

"You better watch it, Suri. What's the difference, anyway? She's the boss," another black suit added as he spit a lump of tobacco into a small cup.

Mr. Suri was silent.

"I had a childhood friend—her name was Nadia Cherkovskaya, not Tamovsky, but there are many Nadias in Russia," I said. My stomach turned with the memory of Nadia and Pepe.

The gentleman spit into the cup again. "It's chewing tobacco, a bad habit, but I can't give it up," he admitted when he noticed I was staring.

"You're going to get cancer of the mouth," another fellow with a high-pitched voice added.

"Hey, the boss ain't no man, that's for sure." Everyone laughed as the spitter indicated with his arms the ample chest with which she was endowed.

"I believe the name would be Tamovskaya, for a lady," I said.

I heard a car door slam. Mr. Suri went to look out the window but was restrained.

"Sit!" said the smallest of the lot, who was wearing black patent leather shoes with wedged heels.

"Her nickname is 'Treasure Chest,'" the spitter added.

"Hey, Bacco, don't go disrespecting Big N," said a fellow with thick hands.

"She told me she likes that name," he added.

"Russian women are very proud of their bodies," I said.

The door to the office opened.

"Yes, we are proud," said the person coming through the door.

"Welcome, boss, we were just finishing up with Mr. Suri," the gentleman with the mustache said.

"Who is this?" she asked, looking at me.

"A fellow comrade. Stalina is her name."

It was Nadia. My Nadia.

"I knew a Stalina when I was young," she said as she turned to look at me.

Our eyes took focus. The age lines did not keep us from recognizing an old acquaintance. A small line of a scar at the edge of her left chin was all that remained of Pepe's bite. Nadia carried herself with importance and elegance in a tailored black suit. Her hair was long and wavy and a couple of shades lighter than I remembered. Her lips were perfectly lined with pencil and filled in with a deep red lipstick.

"I am Stalina Folskaya," I said in Russian.

"Stalina, I know who you are. I like your hair; the color black suits you. What are you doing here?" she added in English.

"It's a long story," I replied in Russian.

"She works here," Mr. Suri piped in.

"Yes, I run the front desk and design the rooms," I added in Russian.

"The rooms of this motel have a reputation. The other motels, my motels, are losing business because of them," she said in Russian.

We continued in our native tongue.

"Did you get married, or is that an alias?" I asked.

"I married an American, of Russian descent, to get my papers. He is out of my life now. It did not work out."

"Business is business," I said.

"Yes, it is. I am buying Mr. Suri out. I need the income. I want all the motels; my parents still depend on me."

"Maybe your motels need something besides 'lunchtime specials.' Where are your parents?" I asked.

The black suits were getting agitated with our conversation in Russian.

"Brighton Beach. Where they all are," she said and then turned to the fellow with the widow's peak. "Frank…"

"Yes, boss?"

"Give Mr. Suri the money," she said in English.

"Mr. Suri, what's going on?" I asked.

"Stalina, I'll be leaving. Madame N is giving me an offer I can't refuse. Garson and I are moving to Arizona. There are business opportunities in the desert. Chander and his mother live there. I want to be closer to him. The money will help. I'm sorry, Stalina," he said, holding the leather satchel to his chest.

The money and valise gave off a strong swampy odor.

"Your boss had plans that would ruin my motels," Nadia said.

My heart sank. I would miss Mr. Suri. Bacco spit again into the cup.

"This is capitalism, Mr. Suri?" I asked.

"More like extortion. Mara's gone already. She left with that boyfriend to Florida. I found a note. She must have suspected something," he added.

"You two finish up your business. We'll be taking over now," the gentleman with thick fingers said. He wore a pinky ring with a diamond that gave off a flat glint when he waved his hand at us.

"What about me?" I said. "My job? My rooms?"

"Stalina, you stay, run the motel," Nadia said.

"But boss, I thought you said I could run this place," Bacco whimpered.

"Bacco, go outside and clean the pine needles off the boss's car," the man with the pinky ring said.

"But..."

"Stalina will be an asset to this establishment, and anyway I owe her," Nadia added.

"You don't owe me anything, Nadia."

"Bad things happened after they put your dog down. It was not your fault."

I said, "I can't believe you still think about that after all these years."

"I still have the scar, and my father took his revenge."

"More than the dog," I said.

Nadia was distracted by one of her men showing her the time on his pocket watch. She did not answer my question.

There was still unfinished business between us, but at the moment I felt inspired and empowered by my new position. I again felt the pang of the loss of Pepe, but I also had a new idea for a room inspired by a formal dining room in the palace at Peterhof. Speaking Russian again gave me the idea. The bed would be made to look like a formal dining table. "Bed-able," I would call it. Chandeliers, hunting murals on the walls, dark purple and green velvets, and many, many mirrors.

"My dream is to have Berlin, Connecticut, become the short-stay capital of the East Coast," Nadia added with great confidence.

"Yes!" her gentlemen all cheered.

Bacco was spitting and grumbling and hesitating to go outside.

"Go on, Bacco, clean the pine needles off the boss's windshield."

"I will serve your ambitions well," I said, and then I turned to Mr. Suri.

"I had no idea Nadia ran the other motels, sir."

"Please don't call me sir, especially now that you're the boss. Maybe that's what you wanted all along."

"Mr. Suri, please, don't. What was it? Was it the drawings?" I asked Nadia.

"It was the drawings," Bacco said.

"Shhh, Bacco, you talk too much. Go out and clean the boss's car before I smack you," the gentleman with the pinky ring said as he boxed him on the side of the head.

"Who saw them?" Mr. Suri asked.

"Go ahead, Bacco, tell him," Nadia said.

"Alfredo from the Kiwanis Club owns a cesspool company. He's my brother-in-law. He scoped out the site for the septic system you wanted to install and saw your drawings under the trees. Progress you wanted. Well, Frank told me that leach field would have made the other motels' cesspools obsolete, and the zoning guy would have to close them down unless they upgraded."

"You're going to have to upgrade at some point," Mr. Suri added.

"The cost, the taxes—business was slow. We never would have survived," Nadia said.

"This place was starting to depress me anyway. I'm going to open a laundromat in Tempe. Everything clean, that's all I want," Mr. Suri said under his breath.

"Mr. Suri, please, I have good feelings here," I said.

"Hey, this place provides an important public service," the gentleman with the pinky ring said.

"I am proud to provide such service," I added.

"Stalina, you are a very unusual woman. I will miss you," Mr. Suri said.

My eyes still stung from the bleach and pine scent, and the inside of my throat swelled as I held back tears.

"Anything else, Mr. Suri? You need to be on your way," Nadia said.

"What about Svetlana and the crow? Did you speak with your veterinarian friend?" I asked.

"Who's Svetlana?" Nadia asked.

"She's a kitten who lives here. She's being weaned by a crow under the pine trees."

"Yes, I spoke with him," Mr. Suri said. "It's most unusual, and the behavior should be documented."

"Take photographs?" I asked

"Photograph it, film it. It is a freak of nature and would be invaluable for research."

"A scientific oddity, like King Kong!" Bacco said.

"Like Jojo the Dog-Faced Boy. Will it make me famous?" Nadia interjected.

She had not changed at all since we were children. She was still an arrogant, self-serving megalomaniac. Jojo was born in Leningrad and was exploited his whole life by his father in the hands of P. T. Barnum. He spoke German, Russian, and English, but he only barked and growled in the sideshow where they exploited his unfortunate deformity. It was strangely comforting to know that Nadia had not changed.

"That cat is going to be famous, and hopefully a good mouser," Mr. Suri said.

"She's gotten lazy with the crow feeding her," I said.

"Worms won't satisfy her for too long. Soon she'll be wanting real meat. Stalina, take pictures before it's too late," he urged.

"Amalia has a film camera. I'm sure I can borrow it."

"You live with Amalia, don't you?" Nadia said.

"I do. How did you know?" I asked.

"She's the dispatcher for the Majik Cleaning Agency. I'm surprised she did not say anything about me. I got this from her," she said as she reached inside her suit to pull out the strap of her brassiere.

I recognized the pink embroidered flower on the small metal ring that joined the satin strap to the elastic adjustable band. This was one of my bras.

She continued in Russian. "It's hard for me to find a bra that fits well and is pretty. Amalia got these from Russia. Most people have no idea what great lingerie we have at home."

I was devastated. How dare she touch my things and help herself to those bras. Those were mine to sell.

"That's strange, we were just talking about you. She never mentioned anything to me," I said.

"She gave me a great price for it. I heard about her husband's death from my sister, very sad. It was good to see her. I was always jealous that she got to wear makeup when we were young. My mother would not let me wear any until I was twenty years old," Nadia said, guiding the strap back into place under her suit jacket.

"My bras…she stole my bras," I said in disbelief.

Nadia acted as if she did not hear me.

"The stupid Soviets made her feel like her husband betrayed her and the whole country," Nadia said. "We all had to leave; life is better here."

Russia betrayed Amalia, and she betrayed me. It was all very Russian.

"They were my salary, my hard-earned…things. She stole from me. Sometimes I miss Petersburg," I said.

"You won't need those bras, Stalina. We'll make money; things will be better."

"Better?"

"We have a short-stay empire to run. Stalina Folskaya, manager/designer. How does that sound?"

Mr. Suri had been silent, but he pulled out a red gift box from the desk drawer and said, "Stalina, remember this? I found it when I was clearing out my things."

"Yes, I do."

It was the box Mara found unopened in the room. He handed it to me.

"I think it's the same as what she is wearing," he said, indicating Nadia's bra.

I opened the box. It was also one of my bras.

"Boss, we've got a lot to do today," interrupted the fellow with the pinky ring. He was looking at his watch again.

"Don't rush us," she said. "Let me see that, Stalina." She turned to me and spoke in Russian. "Is it my size? I have these boys mesmerized by my money and my boobs."

When she said the word *boobs* in English, her red lips pursed. The sound of the word made me laugh and her fellows uneasy. My own breasts swelled slightly.

Mr. Suri faded into the background as he prepared to make his exit. He took his jacket off the hook and then grabbed an uneaten apple and one of the Statue of Liberty postcards from the front desk. He held the suitcase of money between his legs as he put his jacket on. I don't know how much they gave him, but I hope it was enough at least to replace his failing automobile. We held hands for a moment before he walked out the door.

"I'll write, Stalina."

"I have much to thank you for, Mr. Suri."

"I'll miss you, Stalina."

As he walked away, I watched his elegant long legs carry him across the gravel. There was a steady rhythm to his gait, but with a slightly defeated tempo. When he pulled out of the driveway, his Delta '88 coughed and gagged. The drowning gurgle of the car reminded me of how my mother sounded when I left her in Petersburg. They say Arizona is a good place for such human ailments. Mr. Suri and his car disappeared down the hill.

"Is your mother in Brighton Beach like the rest, Stalina?" Nadia asked in Russian as she took the bra out of the box.

"No, actually, she's dead in Petersburg."

"I'm so sorry. This brassiere is not my size. Maybe it will fit you. It's very pretty, but too small."

"Not my size either. It's very small, like Amalia. I'll take it back to her," I said, laughing.

Nadia laughed too. Her dark suits were restless. She gave an order in English.

"Bacco, take Stalina home so she can get her things."

Chapter Nineteen: Leaving Again

My confrontation with Amalia was not pretty.

"I thought you hated Nadia; that's why I never told you I saw her," she said when I exposed her betrayal.

"Didn't you think our paths would cross at some point?" I asked.

"Well, did the surprise of seeing her soften your anger?" Amalia responded. Her logic became more and more twisted.

"I did not hate her; I was sad about my dog. *You* stealing my bras makes me angry. Seeing Nadia again has changed my life."

"For the better?"

"The motel is mine to run," I said.

"She always hated me because of this mark on my face."

"She doesn't hate you. She was just jealous of your makeup."

Amalia was twisting a long strand of her hair and passing it through her mouth. She's done that since she was a little girl.

"I can't believe you stole my bras and sold one to her," I said.

"I did not take your brassieres," she claimed.

"I sold only one, and it wasn't to Nadia," I retorted.

As we continued to argue, Alexi came into the kitchen.

"Alexi, not now please. Stalina and I are having a discussion," Amalia said.

"What's up, ladies? Trouble on the home front?" he said arrogantly and opened the refrigerator.

"Alexi, get your snack and leave," his mother said.

"Are you two fighting about those stupid bras?" he said.

Amalia slapped him on the side of the head.

"Leave him alone," I said. "Let him speak."

"Hey, yeah, Mom, stop it. You told me it was OK to take those bras."

Amalia took an empty pot off the stove and threw it across the kitchen. It struck the side of a wooden chair and chipped off a piece of blue paint. The pot rattled as it spun around before coming to rest on the pink and green linoleum floor. Shosta and Kovich, who had been watching us from the top of the refrigerator, leapt and slid across the kitchen table. We stood motionless as the cats fled the chaos of the kitchen to the safety of the living room and cowered in the four inches between the couch and the wall.

Alexi broke the silence. "She said you brought those bras for us to sell."

"How could you lie to him like that, Amalia? You made your son an accomplice?" I said. "I should call the police."

"What about your citizenship test, Stalina? You don't want anything messy to interfere with becoming an American."

My citizenship hearing was soon. I wanted to be an American. Amalia hated me for this. She was like my mother and held tightly to her nostalgia for "Mother Russia." I was furious, but I still felt sorry for all she had been through.

Survival by betrayal was for our family and
friends love with a feral scalpel.

This line from one of my father's poems came to mind. I understood and could almost forgive my complicated friend, Amalia. In any case, I needed a place of my own; as roommates our time had come to a close.

"And those porcelain cats of yours..." She stopped and spit into the sink.

"What about them?"

"Don't worry, I would never touch those ugly babies of bourgeois indulgence."

"Bourgeois? What about all your glass miniatures?" I said.

"You can see through glass; there is nothing hidden. It is open and honest, like a peasant. Porcelain is for pigs," she replied. "You are such a traitor."

"The porcelain is beautiful and lifelike, and those brassieres were my last month's salary from the lab."

Alexi had started to back out of the kitchen. "I'm sorry, Stalina. She told me you brought those bras to help us pay the bills."

Soon he would have to start shaving. His mustache had started to grow. It was just a scraggly line of hairs along his upper lip. It looked as if someone had cut off a bit of frayed rug fringe and stuck it up there.

"I don't blame you, Alexi."

Amalia sat down.

"I am moving out," I told Amalia after Alexi had left and I heard the door to the basement slam shut.

"Where will you go, Princess America?"

"I'll live at the motel."

"Ungrateful capitalist!"

"Better to be a thief?" I asked.

"Those are Soviet bras; they belong to us all. By the way, I spoke with Olga this afternoon. She said to call her."

"Why didn't you tell me?"

"You did not give me a chance; you were so upset about your silly bras."

"Those are my bras. The money is mine."

"Get out of my house."

I opened my pink wallet and pulled out three twenty-dollar bills.

"Here, take some Andrew Jacksons, seventh president of the United States, my adoptive country."

"He killed a man in a duel for saying something nasty about his wife."

"You studied for the exam?"

"The test is stupid. They ask you if you have ever committed a crime for which you were not arrested."

"It's a trick question," I said.

"I take survival very seriously," she added.

"And what about stealing? That's a crime."

"I guess I would have to lie to pass your American citizen test. I'd trust a liar less than a thief. Call Comrade Olga."

I took a breath and remembered that Amalia was also a child of the siege, only she stayed in Leningrad with her parents when I was sent away to Camp Flora. Many people perished around her. For the duration, she did not wear her makeup. Face powder was used to fatten up scraps of wallpaper to make gruel. People would stare at the mark on her face, and that's when she would steal a watch or a ring.

The black market was stronger than ever during those nine hundred days.

"A diamond ring could get you a loaf of bread," she once told me.

"What's the sixty dollars for?" she asked.

"Partial rent—it's only the first week of the month. Take it."

I went to pack my bag. The stairs creaked as I climbed, and my sneakers sounded like a hungry baby bird as they hit linoleum. Shoes with rubberized soles are a wonderful invention. With them on, even when I am feeling low, my feet are up.

My room, my *terem*, had a single cot and a bedside table with a lamp with a monkey eating a banana on the base topped with a yellow and white striped shade. When I first moved in it made me laugh. Everything in the house was oddly thrown together. The cuckoo clock. The one wooden blue chair in the kitchen. Nothing matched. Could it be that everything in the house was stolen? Many of the things I needed to pack were on a set of shelves Amalia made for me. The shelves were separated and propped up with various objects: a cement cupid figurine, a broken stereo speaker, and several flowerpots. I slid my suitcase out from under the cot and opened it. It was empty except for one of the bras that Alexi had left untouched. Size 85D—in America that's a 44D. A good-sized brassiere. He'd removed the porcelain cats from the cups of the bras and tucked them into the side pockets. I was glad they were safe. I wouldn't sell this bra. I might use it for decoration in one of the rooms at the motel. A "Lingerie Fantasy Room" would be very enticing, I thought. My nose tingled. There was a tickling remaining scent of home—Petersburg—lingering in the shadows of the suitcase.

I began removing things from the shelves. On top was the photograph of my mother and father on the porch from when I was thirteen. The glass in the frame was covered with a thin film of dust. I drew circles in it revealing my mother's hands, then her face, under the dust. A tear fell from the corner of my right eye and landed on my father's face. I passed my thumb through the droplet to clean the rest of the glass. I had never noticed before that my mother's right index finger was bandaged, and there was blood seeping through the gauze. I don't remember my mother cutting her finger, but it was probably still throbbing when the picture was taken. She made a cherry pie the day the photograph was taken. Maxim visited and ate pie with us. Amalia and I played cards. My father read his leather-bound copy of *Julius Caesar*, the same one I was packing from c shelves. As Maxim walked up the steps of the porch, my father read a quote from the play, never lifting his eyes off the page.

Brutus, I do observe you now of late.
I have not from your eyes that gentleness
And show of love as I was wont to have.
You bear too stubborn and too strange a hand
Over your friend that loves you.

* * *

"Good evening, Leonid," Maxim had said that evening as he came up the steps. "Reading your favorite play, I see."

My father did not answer.

"Hello, Maxim, would you like a glass of tea?" my mother asked him.

"Tea, thank you, Sophia," Maxim said to my mother.

My father said nothing, got up from his chair, and went into the house. Amalia had put down her last card, winning the hand. "Let's play another," she said.

We played, but I was distracted and lost the next three hands. I could hear my father pacing and my mother rattling pans in the kitchen. Maxim sat on the steps and smoked cigarette after cigarette. The smoke filled the porch. My mother stepped through the smoke cloud with Maxim's tea and a piece of pie. She pulled the cigarette from his mouth so he could eat, and he watched as she drew the smoke into her lungs and released it around him. He devoured the pie but never took his eyes off her. They walked off the porch into the evening, sharing another cigarette. Amalia won another hand. My father stayed inside. My mother returned alone. In the meantime, I had finally won a hand.

"You girls should be in bed by now," she said.

"Stalina finally won. One more hand so we can tie," Amalia pleaded with my mother.

"You're a good friend, Amalia. Now go to bed, girls," my mother said.

"Where's your father?" Amalia asked.

"Asleep in his chair," I told her.

My mother went inside.

"Girls, come in now. I'll let you skip your baths if you go right up to bed."

We left our playing cards and went upstairs. In the living room my father was unconscious in his chair with his teacup knocked over in his lap. There was a stain on his pants where the liquid had soaked into the worsted wool. My mother was standing in the doorway to the kitchen, smoking another cigarette. I could not see her face in the shadows.

When we got upstairs, Amalia asked, "Your parents don't touch anymore, do they?"

I could not remember the last time I saw them touch each other.

"They don't need to touch," I told her.

"Everyone needs to touch," she said.

* * *

I finished packing and went downstairs. Amalia was in the basement with Alexi. They were having an argument. I picked up the phone to call Olga in Russia, but the smell of cigarettes and gardenia perfume on the receiver made me sick to my stomach. Bacco was waiting in a car to take me back to the motel. My new home.

* * *

I reached Olga from the office phone on the first try. She had been to the rooming house earlier in the day and learned the details of my mother's passing from one of her roommates.

"I hope you don't mind, but I told them I was you," she said.

"Who did you speak with?"

"Ludmilla was her name. She said she thought I was shorter and had darker hair. I told her I had only recently become a blond and was wearing heels."

"I remember Ludmilla. She had the cot across from my mother, and her son used to bring her chocolates."

"Is he married?" Olga was constantly on the lookout for men with connections. She continued, "Chocolates at the salon would be nice for treats."

"Ludmilla never had the heart to tell her son that the chocolates gave her indigestion. She gave them away to the nurses and kitchen staff. My mother used to complain that Ludmilla got special attention because of the chocolates. She told me, 'They gave her an extra piece of chicken the other day. Maybe you could do something for me, Stalina?' That was when I gave her the toilet tissue and gifted the brassieres to the nurse."

Olga explained, "Ludmilla told me that evening noodle soup with fish balls was served in the commissary for dinner. When the bowl was placed in front of your mother, she picked up one of the balls with her spoon, flung it against the wall, and screamed, 'Capitalist pigs! They hoard the caviar for themselves and let us eat this slop!' The nurses tried to calm her down with a cup of tea. She apologized for the bad behavior and assured them she was actually fond of fish balls, but had been possessed by a bad memory."

I told Olga, "Mother must have been thinking of the time when Nadia's parents were giving a party and served caviar. She left the party and went behind their house with a full mouth. I ran after her, thinking she was ill. She spit out the caviar and said, 'I feel like I just sucked the cock of a KGB operative.' Nadia's dog, Trala, came out and started barking at us. 'Are you the house informant?' she said and spit at the yapping poodle. 'That would figure.' 'Mother, it's just a dog,' I said. Then a stray cat with a split ear crawled out from under the house and began to lick the caviar from the leaves of the hydrangea where it had landed. We went back to the party, leaving the cat picking at the bits that got caught between her claws. 'That must be Ezhov; he was known for licking Stalin's ass,' Mother said about the cat. 'Mother, it's just a stray cat,' I assured her."

Olga described how she'd been told. Mother's roommates had returned from dinner only to find her standing at the edge of her bed facing the picture of my father—the one with the shovel. With red lipstick she had scrawled these lines on the starched white bedsheet:

The last time we were
Together we watched as the ice cream
Slowly dripped onto our daughter's finely manicured hands.
I don't care for chocolate, but it is ecstasy for her.
The hysteria of you is a charm
Not mine alone.
I cannot protect you from the Sun,
But you can love us all.

This was another poem of my father's we found amongst his things. According to Ludmilla, the roommates stood by their respective cots, chanted the words, and were soon dancing around the room swinging in one another's arms.

Frieda, who has one leg shorter than the other, got up on her cot and challenged the room, "In what year did Leonid write that poem?"

Many knew my father's work; I made sure his poems were passed among other poets and friends.

"If I know, do I win something?" asked Talia, the shy one who had long gray braids.

"It was like we were children again," Ludmilla told Olga. "Then the nurses came and made everyone go to bed. Your mother refused to have the sheet changed, so with the words draped over her body, she went to sleep, fully dressed."

Olga went on to explain how the rest of the night unfolded. Lights-out was ten o'clock. Around three in the morning, Ludmilla heard my mother talking. She had taken the photograph of my father off the wall, laid it next to her on the pillow, and was whispering to it.

"Is everything all right?" Ludmilla asked my mother.

There was no answer, but my mother continued talking to the photograph. Ludmilla heard her crying and was about to get up when my mother sat up and reached her arms out as if to embrace someone. Her face was filled with a big broad smile, and then her eyes closed. She fell back onto the bed, barely making a sound. Ludmilla waited for my mother to move, but she remained still.

"Ludmilla said it was as if someone had come to greet her," Olga said.

I wonder who it was. Maxim? My father? It was a relief to hear she was happy about whoever or whatever had taken her to the other side.

"Could it be that you get to spend eternity with the person you truly love?" I asked Olga.

"Now wouldn't that be a kick in the pants. Having to wait till you die to be happy. What a silly plan," Olga said. "It would be nice to have some happiness while we're here."

I had nothing to say, but I thought about how nice it would be to spend an eternity with Trofim.

* * *

As I spoke with Olga, the weather changed dramatically. The temperature dropped and the rain turned to icy snow. Three geraniums in the window box under the office window, surprised by the cold and ice, went top-heavy and touched the dirt. The whitening branches of the pine trees looked very Russian.

"Is there snow in Petersburg?" I asked Olga.

"What a question, Stalina. There's been snow on the ground since October," she replied.

I heard a dog yapping in the background. "Is that a dog?" I asked.

"That's Neptune. I found him near the Neva by the Admiralty, shivering in the cold."

"Neptune?"

"He fell into the sewer. It's a miracle he survived, so I thought I'd give him an impressive name. He's actually very small."

"It's a big bark he has. Are they keeping the metro stations warm?" I asked.

"Yes, of course, like always, and we still go there to meet after work," she said, "like always."

She laughed, and I cried.

"Stalina, why don't you come and retrieve your mother's things? You don't have to give anything up. Just come."

"It's too soon. I am trying to be happy here."

"And what about here? Many things will never change, but everything feels different. That's almost like happiness."

"Here it is about the pursuit of happiness, and that is what I want."

"You could do that anywhere, Stalina."

"The motel brings me happiness. It's mine now."

"Did you kill your boss? Did you marry him?"

"Did you know Nadia is here?" I asked.

"Did she have her boss eliminated? I heard she has adjusted to America very easily."

"She arranged for me to have the motel; she's in the business."

"You, beholden to Nadia. Stalina, I think you should come home. You don't want her to own you."

"She's letting me do as I please. Olga, you could open a hair salon here," I added.

"We both have our hands dipped in darkness, Stalina. You with Nadia, and I get my supplies from the black market. Everything they do happens behind a door, as they say, and my beauty salon provides the perfect façade. I always have plenty of hair spray, shampoo, and polish. Otherwise, my business would be nothing."

"It's not so different here, but I like the motel life. It suits me."

"Send Nadia my regards. I never thought you would be friends."

"It's not about friendship, it's about business."

"Stalina, where should I mail your mother's things? Tell me quickly, I need to take Neptune for his walk."

I looked out the window and saw Svetlana's crow digging in the snow under the pine trees. "I have a kitten named Svetlana," I said.

"Only one? What's the address, Stalina?"

I picked up a card from the front desk and read the address to her. The Liberty Motel, 345 Windsor Avenue, Berlin, Connecticut, 06037. Mr. Suri's and his brother's names were still on the card. I crossed out their names and wrote "Stalina Folskaya, Manager/Designer" and added "Rooms for the Imaginative" underneath.

* * **

Olga called me back the next day.

"Bad news, Stalina. I can't send the ashes."

"But it's my mother. Did they find out you weren't me? People die away from home all the time."

"She was home, Stalina. You are the one who is away."

"You just need a certificate of death—the rooming house should have it—and an affidavit from the crematorium stating the ashes are those of the deceased."

"It's not that. Someone else picked up her ashes."

I was not sure I heard her correctly.

"The rooming house said your mother had a visitor. A man."

"He came often?"

"He came the day after she died and paid for the cremation."

"I sent them two hundred dollars for the expenses. Who was this person?"

"It was an M. Kharkovsky who signed the register."

"Maxim."

"You know him?"

"He was my uncle, sort of."

"A relative? Then it's easy; he could help you."

"He's not my uncle."

"A friend to your mother?"

"Yes, and I called him uncle." It never occurred to me that anyone else would be sad about my mother's passing.

"I have his address, Stalina. The rooming house gave it to me."

"He probably still lives in the same place, 45 Smolny Prospekt."

"Yes, that's the place."

20 February 1994
Dear Maxim,

It's been a long time since we have had contact, but I heard from my friend Olga, who has helped me since my mother's passing, that you are in possession of her ashes. I also learned that you paid for her cremation. That was very generous, but the rooming house on Lermontovsky Prospekt has cheated us both. I sent two hundred U.S. dollars for the expenses. Olga went to pick up Mother's ashes and her few personal things to send them to me here in the U.S. where I now live. It is not an option for me to travel to Russia at the moment to collect them. I am merely a worker at a motel in Berlin, Connecticut, and have not amassed any kind of a fortune, even though I am very happy. I am sorry if you have suffered for the loss of my mother. You meant a great deal to her. Before I left Petersburg, I had a conversation with my mother about her ashes. Here is that conversation word for word. I thought it would amuse you and would help you to carry out her wishes.

"Mother, your ashes, what would you like me to do with your ashes?"

"My ass? Why are you so concerned with my ass, Stalina? There are nurses here."

"*Not your ass, Mother, your ashes, after you die. Do you have any requests?*"

"*I'm not dead yet.*"

"*Mother, the time will come, and I just want to do what is right.*"

"*Use them to powder your face. You are always so concerned about your looks.*"

"*What about where we used to swim in the gulf?*"

"*That water is polluted.*"

Maxim, did you not find my mother infuriating toward the end?

"*Mother, I have many memories of swimming with you there. The beautiful gardens and fountains of the Winter Palace in the background. The fried fish sandwiches we used to have for a picnic. It was a pretty place, wasn't it, Mother?*"

Maxim, I know you are not my uncle. It was on one of our swims that my mother told me about you.

"*Then put me in the sea, Stalina, if that's what you want.*"

"*Is there someplace else?*"

"*I want revenge, Stalina.*"

"*With your ashes? For whom?*"

"*Find Nadia's parents; spread me in their midst. I want to harass them for all time. They don't deserve any peace.*"

"*I am not sure where they are, Mother.*"

"*Find them. They had your father sent away.*"

"*How do you know that, Mother?*"

"*They were both informers. Radya used to say she got all that caviar and fine wine from a cousin who worked on a ship. It was all arranged.*"

I know where Nadia's parents are, Maxim. They live here in America in the Brighton Beach. You may keep some of her ashes, spread some in the Gulf of Finland, and send the rest to me to take to Brighton at the beach.

Yours truly,

Stalina Folskaya, Sophia's daughter

He wrote back. Quickly.

Dear Stalina,

Your letter came today, and I write to you as I await my dinner at the Café Karenina, near the Maryinsky Theater. Perhaps you know the place. Your mother and I had dinner here often. I will go to the opera this evening. Carmen *is playing. The maître d' led me to a table in a corner from which I have the advantage to view the entire restaurant. Each table is decorated with a white linen cloth, a small white vase, and a fresh cut yellow rose. I want to set the scene for you, Stalina, because if you are anything like your mother, you will love all the details.*

The vaulted ceiling of the café is painted with elaborate medieval-style tapestry hunting scenes. Knights on horseback in full armor pursuing unicorns and lions with wings. The restaurant was originally called "The Gryphon and the Unicorn," but Leo Tolstoy supposedly ate here and enjoyed himself tremendously, so the owners renamed it Café Karenina. The paintings are still a tourist attraction, of almost equal popularity as the famous beef goulash. The original owner's twin daughters painted the murals and were renowned for their ability to paint a canvas simultaneously without speaking about its contents.

The waiter has delivered my stew and refilled my wine glass. I thank you for offering me a portion of your mother's ashes. I will spread some in the Gulf of Finland as per her request. I will use my few connections to get the documents needed to safely send the ashes to you. Expect them soon. I hear Brighton Beach in the winter can be very much like Leningrad, only a bit warmer. It is up to you to honor your mother's request to spread her ashes near Nadia's parents. Revenge is a strange animal. The past does not change. They were wrong to give your father up. An easy target because he wrote poetry when he was angry and wore that odd chapeau. I am much more passive, and that could be the reason your father tolerated me. He knew I would be there for your mother. It was difficult for us all, but please know that I did my best to make her happy.

I have your mother's copy of Through the Looking Glass. *We used to read it to each other. The pages still smell of her rose attar perfume. If you don't mind, I would like to keep the book. She must have held it after holding a leaky ink pen because her thumbprint is smudged permanently onto the first page. If I remember correctly, this book was also a favorite of yours.*

I am deeply sorry for your loss.

Sincerely,
Maxim K.

I can see why my mother loved Maxim, but I think he may be mistaken about the thumbprint. My father's fingers were always covered in ink from his writing. His thumbprint decorated the first page of my copy of the same book. I know the beginning of the story from memory.

"Chapter One, Looking Glass House. One thing was certain, that the white kitten had had nothing to do with it—it was the black kitten's fault entirely. For the white kitten had been having its face washed by the old cat for the last quarter of an hour (and bearing it up pretty well considering): so you see it couldn't have had any hand in the mischief."

When my father read about the naughty kitten unraveling the ball of yarn Alice had been tending to in the quiet of the afternoon, he made it all seem so real. It was snowing in the story, just like it is here today. Alice thought the snow hitting the windows sounded like kisses. "Just as if someone was kissing the window all over outside," she told the kitten as she settled in for her famous nap.

* * *

Here at the Liberty Motel, Svetlana has grown full and round in the care of the crow under the pines. I named the crow Zarzamora, like my hair dye from Cuba. I like to call her ZZ for short. Svetlana goes out every day to see her, even though I have started to leave food for her in the linen room. She goes out when it snows to visit with ZZ even though there are no worms to be had from the frozen ground. When Svetlana walks in the snow, she shakes out her paws every couple of steps as she makes her way toward the pine trees. After some initial squawking and mewling, both animals settle down and sit together quietly. They linger. The cat's nose and the bird's beak twitch when they smell something on the wind. A car coming up the drive, or the linen room door opening, interrupting their business of shuffling through pine needles to find slow bugs. I started taking photographs of these two, but it felt like I was intruding. I have no desire to exploit their love. Leave the lovers alone. This is the policy I have adopted for my customers at the Liberty as well.

Chapter Twenty: To Come Again

My mother's ashes arrived from Maxim in a cigar box wrapped in the yellow apron my mother always wore. The pockets were decorated with traditional embroidery in red, yellow, and blue dancers skipping along the front of the apron. My father bought it for her when he was on a trip to Warsaw. She wore it every day, taking it off only when she went to bed. She often looked at aprons sold in the markets, but she never purchased a new one. Maxim included a note with his package.

Dear Stalina,

 As you know, your mother, Sophia, was very dear to me, and I mourn her passing. I visited her even when she did not recognize me anymore. I have taken care to spread her ashes in the Gulf of Finland. The days are getting a little longer now, and I had a sunny afternoon for the travel to Peterhof. There were people swimming in the gulf even though the temperature was close to freezing. The cold water does not appeal to me, but the swimmers all looked vigorous and pleased with themselves. Your mother was a wonderful swimmer. There may have been someone swimming that day who swam with her at the Academy. I threw her ashes out across the top of the water. They stayed on the surface and formed a cloud that changed shapes as the current moved back and forth. I stood at the water's edge and watched as the cloud of ashes first came toward me and then drifted steadily out to sea. The small, gentle waves were like your mother's elegant, long-armed strokes taking her farther and farther away from shore.

One of the nurses at the rooming house told me that the night your mother died, there was some confusion over fish balls in the commissary. She became hysterical and threw them across the room. They brought her back to her room to calm down. She put on this apron, which she had hidden under her mattress, and demanded that the staff let her do the cooking. They finally calmed her down by offering her a lipstick. She painted her lips and then used the lipstick to write something on her bedsheet. There is a mark on the apron where she patted her lips. I thought you might like to have the apron. Your mother was a wonderful cook. I hope you learned her recipe for cherry pie, which was a favorite of mine. It is good to know you seek happiness in America. This concept seems very foreign, but very commendable, if not a bit lovely and naive.

Nostrovya,
Maxim K.

* * *

I was surprised Maxim did not know the poem my mother wrote on her top sheet. I did not want to break the spell of his ardor. Maybe the people at the rooming house knew he was not her husband and hid my father's words from him. I was inspired by his story of the ashes and was excited to be taking them to their requested liberation.

"I have to go to New York to pick up my mother's ashes. There is some regulation," I explained to Nadia. Maxim had in fact sent them to me directly, but I lied to Nadia. "I also want to take this opportunity to see the Statue of Liberty, and if I have time I will go to Brighton."

"The Statue of Liberty—I have only seen it in pictures. It will be good for you to see Brighton Beach. My parents will be happy to have you visit."

Revenge is filled with subversion like a blini stuffed with mushrooms.

Nadia continued, "They will walk you along the board-walk and you will see the ocean."

"I would like that."

"Take a day away from the motel; you have been working without a break. I'll have one of my boys cover for you."

"Thank you, I could use a day off. It has been a hard time for me," I said.

Perhaps Nadia had no idea how her parents betrayed mine.

"Stalina, what happened with you and Amalia?"

"She stole something of mine from Russia, sold it, and believed it was her right to do so. There was no place for me with her anymore. I am happy living at the motel."

"Have you heard from Mr. Suri?"

"Yes, a postcard came the other day."

I showed Nadia the postcard of a rodeo in a shopping mall in Oklahoma. At one end of the rodeo ring there was a ten-foot-high model of the Statue of Liberty. Mr. Suri's handwriting was small, tight, and very delicate.

Dear Stalina,

On the way to Arizona, I made a stop in Oklahoma. Garson has joined me here to complete the journey together. The replica of Lady Liberty reminded me of the motel and you. Maybe you should get one for the entrance. I am fascinated by the rodeo. Taming the wild beast. I bought a cowboy hat, and Garson got a whip. Whatever happened to Svetlana and the crow? Does the life of a motel manager suit you? I'm sure it does. If you still think of me, I hope it is as a friend. I will send my address when I arrive at my destination.

Yours truly,
Franklin Suri

"He really cared for you, Stalina," Nadia said after reading the card.

"I liked him very much; he was hardworking," I said.

"I hope I didn't stop anything between you two, but he was ruining my business."

"I think he is happier now that he has gotten away from the motel. I don't think he was a true believer in the short-stay concept."

"Not like us! Short stays forever!"

"Short stays forever!" I joined in.

"Our customers return for their short stays, over and over," she said.

"They come and hope to…" I stopped and waited for Nadia to join me.

"To come! And come again!" She laughed and threw her arms overhead and then embraced me. Two days later, I took a day off from work.

Chapter Twenty-one: Brighton Beach

Once in New York City, I traveled by subway to Brighton Beach. Compared to our glorious Russian metro, the New York subway was like a creature suffering from a bad case of gastric distress coupled with rheumatoid arthritis. The tunnels were intestines, and the screeching brakes were the beast's twisted, grinding jaw. When the doors opened, a belch of rancid smell permeated the car. Crazed writings in a strange alphabet covered the walls, and garbage was everywhere. A lonesome, unattended roaring giant was this train named N of the BMT Line. All of this was very unsavory, but as the train came out of the tunnel, I was delighted to see a beautiful view of the homes and narrow streets of Brooklyn. On top of one building was a billboard for a hairdresser written in Cyrillic. I felt a thrill and fear, as if I was returning home. It was a Monday in March and, coincidentally, the anniversary of Stalin's death. Anyone alive in Russia at the time remembers where they were on that day in 1953. I was at home with Olga, playing cards and admiring our new hairstyles in the hand mirror my mother gave me for my birthday. As I came down from the elevated subway platform at Brighton Beach Avenue, the busy markets and businesses reminded me of home. The smell of juniper, cinnamon, and dill used to pickle beets, turnips, and garlic, along with the mouth-watering oils from the smoked fish, filled the air along the sidewalks. Who could resist going inside the markets? And Russian was being spoken on the street. Surrounded by everything familiar, I felt light in the head.

"I'm meeting Mina at three at the hairdresser," a woman wearing a gray sable coat said in Russian to another woman in mink.

"The meringue cake at M&I is fresh today. Do you want me to pick you up some?"

"If it's not too much trouble, I would love some for tea. My mother-in-law is coming over, and the meringue cake is her favorite."

"Sweetening her up again?" the woman in mink asked.

"Josip and I are going on the cruise we won at the raffle. I want her to mind the dogs while we're gone."

"Meringue cake will do it?"

"That and if we promise to take her on the next cruise."

They turned the corner. I watched as their coats disappeared into a fruit stand, and I headed for the boardwalk. Even a block away the damp salt smell of the sea hung in the air. The wood of the boardwalk was wet from a morning rain. I sat on a bench against a newly whitewashed wall and stared at the ocean. An old woman wearing a paisley headscarf was throwing bread over a railing, feeding seagulls on the beach. The birds were going in circles overhead. A young mother pushing a baby carriage stopped to wipe mustard off her child's hands and face. The sun was warm and lovely, and the seagulls threw shadows like airplanes flying in formation over the boardwalk. Two painters were whitewashing the walls along the sides of the boardwalk. They stopped to take a break when their partner returned with a tray of hot dogs and french fries. I could smell the food on the wind. The child with the mustard on his face started crying. His mother lit a cigarette and pushed the stroller closer to the beach and the seagulls. The birds screeched in harmony with the baby. There was much commotion as the birds rose, flapping fiercely and surrounding the old woman. She dumped the remaining crumbs in her bag over the railing, sat back, and fixed her scarf, which had come undone. The child started laughing, and the mother put out her cigarette and continued to walk down the board-walk. The birds made a spiral into the air and dove for the bread. Brighton Beach was feeling very agreeable.

A dog came running up the boardwalk as the painters started to whitewash the next wall. The owner held out a large bone to the dog, who promptly grabbed it and put it securely between his front paws. He chewed ravenously right in front of me. His owner, who was wearing a blue and red jogging outfit and had a little bit of a limp, came over to retrieve his dog.

"Come on, Pepe, I haven't finished my run," he said.

The dog ignored him. This was one of the largest dogs I had ever seen. He had long legs with bulging joints. His back had black splotches on his otherwise white coat. He had haunches the size of a pony and did not sit his behind fully on the slats of the boardwalk. A large but delicate beast.

"I had a dog named Pepe. He was much smaller than yours," I said.

The man was dark like Mr. Suri and had a gold ring in his nose.

"He's a Great Dane, and he loves to run on the beach."

"Mine liked to run along the river."

"The Hudson?" he asked.

"No, the Neva, at home."

"The Neva?" he asked.

"It's in Russia, St. Petersburg."

"So many people from Russia live here. Did your Pepe like to chase his shadow on the beach like this one?" he said, laughing.

"Dogs are so easily fooled," I said.

"They may be small-brained, but they are forever loyal," he added.

"Loyalty, yes, it's their nature," I said.

The whole time we spoke, the man jogged in place.

"Good day, ma'am, we must be on our way. Come along, Pepe," he said as he tipped his cap with an *N* and a *Y* embroidered on it and ran down the boardwalk in the direction of a giant Ferris wheel and an Eiffel Tower–looking structure. Pepe loped behind with the bone dangling from his jaws. The sun was bright and harsh shining off the panting dog's white coat.

On the beach, broken glass and plastic bags had settled down into the hardened winter sand mixed with snow and the occasional clamshell. A man with hair down to his shoulders was flying a kite with very little success. The seagulls were still crying and fighting over whatever bread was left. The bird sounds and squeals from children were picked up by the wind, stretched and muffled by the dull sound of the waves. Beach sounds were the same in Russia. The Baltic and the Atlantic must merge at some point, even here at Brighton Beach.

Russians were easy to spot, even from a distance. The head shawls, the way they leaned back and forth when they spoke to each other. Babushkas listening to babushkas.

The man's kite was finally flying, and the wind was making his hair flutter around his head. He was running backwards to keep the kite in the air. He was headed straight for the boulders of a breakwater. I didn't think he could see where he was going.

"Excuse me, sir!" I yelled. "Watch out! You are going to hit the…"

Too late. He was down and the kite was in the surf. He was getting up. He brushed himself off. He looked embarrassed even though he did not know that anyone saw him take the fall. He probably never heard my warning. No witnesses, no embarrassment, only a kite floating on the ocean's waves, and no need for me to impose myself on everyone I encountered. *Move on, Stalina, you have more important business to attend to.*

The boardwalk stretched up and down the beach, curved with the shape of the coastline. As I walked closer to the Ferris wheel, I could also see an amusement park rising up behind the boardwalk. One hot dog seller was open. All the other stands had metal gates pulled down. They advertised clams on the half shell, cotton candy, and popcorn. There was a roller coaster! I would have taken a ride in honor of my room design, but it appeared to be closed for the season. The clouds at the horizon were moving along with me. The Ferris wheel was in sight. There was a howling sound coming from somewhere in the amusement park. As I got closer to the source, I could hear that it was coming from a tower. A tower that was a ride that took people up and up to see everything around Brighton and out to sea. The wind was whipping inside of it, making a very mournful sound. There was an observation deck around the tower that slid up and down like a ring on a finger.

That deck moving up and down made me think how my mother would obsessively slide her wedding ring up and down her finger after my father was taken away. She had become very thin and would remove it to wash the dishes so as not lose it down the drain. Her fingers once were chubby and the ring was held tight by the soft bulge of flesh that used to form below her knuckle. The very day that Stalin died, Olga gave me a black ribbon for my hair.

"It's for mourning because you are his namesake, Stalina," Olga said as we stood in front of the mirror and she styled my hair with the ribbon.

After Olga left I took off the ribbon, and as my mother washed dishes, I strung her ring on the ribbon and tied it around her neck. That's where she wore it from then on. There were people crying in the streets for days after Stalin died. My mother was very quiet, there were no tears, but when she washed the dishes, she let the water run over the rationed legal limit.

* * *

The tower continued its song of lament as I walked back to Brighton Beach Avenue. I passed a market that sold handmade brooms just like ones the street cleaners in Russia used to keep the avenues spotless. I had not seen one since I left.

"I'll take one of these," I said in Russian to the man standing in front of the store.

He wore a fedora covered in a shower cap, and he did not respond to me, so I picked up the broom. "What do you want a broom like that for?" he finally said.

"They do the job of two brooms at once," I replied.

"That's ridiculous. I just have them for the old ladies. They never stop sweeping; it's not the broom that does the job of two."

"Perhaps," I said.

"Not that I don't want to make a sale. I'll sell you two for one, just because it's starting to rain," he said.

"I'd rather not carry them back on the bus to Connecticut."

"Connecticut? Fancy, aren't we?"

"It's where I live. I am a tourist here." I started to make my way down the block.

"Hey, Connecticut," he called after me, "if you lived here, you'd be home by now. No broom for you? How will you keep your *foyer* clean?"

He laughed. I could still hear him laughing when I turned into another store.

M&I Grocers was one of the bigger markets located under the trestle of the subway. Walking through the doors I saw many of the things we missed back home in Russia. Guilty pleasures of smoked fish, farmer cheese, ice creams. Sausages. Things that were very expensive and difficult, even with money, to come by. Braided challah breads, squid salad, pickled tomatoes, and more.

I walked up the curved white metal stairs to a balcony and a beautiful café. At the counter the cakes for the day were all lined up. There was the meringue cake that the women on the street had spoken about, and a plum cake with walnuts and buttercream icing. Behind the counter, a tall blond-haired fellow in a white uniform asked me in Russian what I wanted.

"Pavashta, cake and coffee with cream," I said and pointed to the plum cake.

"Caf or decaf?" he asked me in English.

"Excuse me?"

"Regular or decaffeinated coffee," he clarified.

"Without caffeine?" I asked.

"Oh, Americans like it that way."

"Maybe I should have a tea instead," I added.

"Your coffee is already poured," he said.

He scowled as I took my cake and coffee and sat at a table. There were mirrors on all the walls and pictures of the owners smiling with Russian dancers and singers. I saw myself in one of the mirrored walls next to a photograph of Vladimir Rashnisky, a crooner who died of alcoholism in 1982. My hair was in great disarray from the wind on the boardwalk. There was Misha Baryshnikov, still so handsome. I saw him perform at the Kirov. His passionate death scene made us all weep. It was a sad day for the ballet when he defected. He must have a very good life here, but there must be things he misses from home, otherwise why would he visit this place.

Chapter Twenty-two: Flying Ashes

The building where Nadia's parents live on Neptune Avenue has a cement path lined with short, spiky, almost dead bushes leading up to two glass doors. It is known as a highrise. We have something similar in Russia, except they are made entirely of cement, and there is rarely a living plant anywhere to be seen.

* * *

"Apartment 15D, *D* as in *do svidaniya*," Nadia told me before I left.

"Shall I call them when I get there?" I asked

"I'll call them before. Don't worry, they will be expecting you," she said.

I wanted Carmela, my new assistant, to run the motel while I was gone. But Nadia insisted on being there with one of her boys to show him how it all worked. The Liberty Motel was still the busiest of all the short-stays on the strip. In my opinion, I had helped to create a good atmosphere at the motel, and our customers liked it enough to return over and over.

"If you have any questions, Carmela will help you. She is learning the business quickly," I assured Nadia.

Carmela was from Nicaragua. She walked up to the motel one day looking for work. I hired her on the spot. Impressed by her assertive nature, I trusted her right away. On her first day, Carmela reorganized the linen room so she could have a desk and a chair to sit at while waiting to clean the rooms. She studied English and wrote letters to her family back home. Svetlana quickly became very attached to her, sitting on a shelf above the desk, watching her every move. The cat followed her from room to room when she cleaned. They had become a very charming team. Carmela also endeared herself to the crow, Zarzamora, by offering her treats of apples and hot dogs. She would let Svetlana out whenever ZZ called for her from under the pine trees.

Carmela said, "That crow is like a jealous lover; she keeps the other crows away when she is with Svetlana."

Carmela read many romance novellas.

* * *

Before pushing the buzzer for 15D, I reached in my bag and touched the pouch with my mother's ashes to remind me of my mission.

"Is that you, Stalina?" a woman's voice yelled in Russian instantly after I pressed the buzzer.

"Yes, that's me. I am here," I answered in Russian.

"Arkady, it's Nadia's friend Stalina," I heard Nadia's mother say as she turned away from the intercom.

Back into the buzzer and even louder than before she said, "Come up, Stalina, fifteenth floor. I'll buzz you in."

"Do you think she knows about us, Radya?" Nadia's father said, not aware that his wife still had a finger on the intercom.

"Yes, I know, Mr. C. That's why I am here," I said as I pushed through the buzzing glass door and saw in my reflection that I had misaligned the buttons of my coat. As I went up in the elevator, I fixed my coat and pulled my hair back.

Arkady and Radya were tiny and crooked with age. Both of them standing side by side barely filled the doorway. The apartment was decorated with glass tables and a couch and chair set made of leather and brass. Not a very cozy place, but then again I was not there seeking comfort.

"Stalina, make yourself comfortable," Radya said, gesturing to a folding chair that had been awkwardly placed between the white leather couch and its bulky matching side chair. I sat and thought for a moment about the last conversation I had with my mother.

"They did not care about anyone but themselves, Stalina," she said. "Under the pretense of being good servants to the state, they were bad Communists. They were not about the people, they were about themselves."

* * *

The view from their living room looked out over the ocean. It was a spectacular sight. I could fall in love with such a view. The sun was breaking through the clouds, and my eyes felt caressed by the light from the ocean. The haze from the rain was disappearing as if the sun were sucking it up like a milkshake through a straw.

"You certainly have a beautiful view," I said.

They both remained standing while I sat. It all felt very awkward.

"Yes, Nadia made sure we had a view, and she had a friend furnish the apartment. It's not quite to our liking, but they say it's very up-to-date. I'll make tea," Radya said.

"I'll help you," I said.

"No need—Arkady likes to do it his way," she said.

Arkady said nothing. They left me alone in the living room on the folding chair. It felt as if they had gone off to discuss how to interrogate a prisoner. I surveyed the apartment to find a place for my mother's ashes. There were several fake potted plants under the windows. My mother detested fake plants almost as much as she hated weak tea. On the mantel there was a collection of glass figurines and an urn. The urn would be perfect for the ashes; that's what urns are for, containing remains. Perched on the mantel, Mother would be able to spy on Radya and Arkady's every move. As they worked in the kitchen, I took the urn down from the mantel to see if anything had already been stored in it. I would have to reconsider if it was already occupied. For instance, Nadia's dog Trala would not be a good bedfellow for my mother. I'm sure that yappy little weasel of a canine was coddled right up till its yappy demise and then given a ceremonious burial. The urn was painted with Chinese figures. Ladies in waiting serving tea to their master. They were dressed in robes of pink, green, and blue. Butterflies and bluebirds flew around their heads. On the bottom there was lettering that I could not decipher. The urn was empty. I pulled out the plastic bag with the ashes and dumped half of them into the urn. A small cloud hung in the air, but it quickly disappeared into the stillness of the room.

"We'll be right out, Stalina," Radya said from the kitchen.

"That's fine. I'm admiring your wonderful view," I said and quickly placed the urn back on the mantel. As I was positioning it, I grazed one of the glass figurines, a ballet dancer in pirouette. The dancer tumbled through the air headfirst and landed unharmed in the plush pile of the white shag carpet. I placed her back on the mantel just as Arkady and Radya were returning from the kitchen. On the side table next to the couch there was a small frame with a photograph of Stalin standing on a bridge with two men at his side. The picture was very familiar. I had a similar one in my collection.

"I was just admiring your glass figures," I said.

My heart was pounding so hard I could see it pumping through my blouse.

"I've been collecting them for years. I like the way the light hits them at different times of the day," Radya said.

"Amalia also collects them," I said.

"Amalia, don't you live with her?" Radya asked.

"I used to," I replied.

She leaned over and whispered to me, "Nadia got me the bra I'm wearing from Amalia. It's one of those sexy ones from home."

"I miss the lingerie from home," I said, still furious.

At that moment the sun was hitting the glass figures from the side and below. The mantel looked like a stage ready for a performance. The bright points of light on the curves and angles of the statues made it appear as if there were footlights. At any moment the orchestra would start to play and the glass dancer, hound dog, snail, grasshopper, and bear would dance around the Cathedral of the Spilled

Blood. Amalia had this very same figurine. The urn was the backdrop around which the players could make their entrances and exits. My mother would be backstage calling all the cues.

Lights fade up.

Arkady put down the tray holding a tea set, some small cakes, and a bowl of sunflower seeds. My father used to eat sunflower seeds when he had tea. The technique for shelling the seeds with his teeth and spitting out just the shell was a highly developed skill.

Tea was poured. I sat on the folding chair with my cup of tea and a slice of lemon cake. Radya sat on the couch by herself. Arkady went to the mantle and pulled the urn from the shelf and took it with him to his chair. Radya got up and gave him a cup of tea and the bowl of sunflower seeds. There was nothing I could do or say. Arkady held the urn under his arm as he popped the first handful of sunflower seeds into his mouth. It took a minute or two before he had shelled the seeds and stored them in his cheek. As he spit the cracked shells into the urn, a cloud of dust instantly formed around his head. I choked on the lemon cake that was halfway down my throat.

"*Ack! Ack!* Radya, what is this? You said you cleaned out the urn!" Arkady screamed and his arms flailed. The cloud of my mother's ashes hung around his head.

"The urn was empty," she said.

I forcibly swallowed the lemon cake and gulped loudly.

"Stalina, take a sip of tea," Radya said. "Was the cake all that hard?"

"I burned my throat earlier on some hot coffee at a bakery. It's still very sensitive," I told her.

"Radya, never mind that. Help me here, take this," Arkady said.

He tried flicking the ashes off his shoulders, but they only became more ground into his shirt and stuck to the tips of his fingers.

"Here, let me help you, Mr. C," I said and grabbed the urn.

"Let me see that, Stalina." Radya grabbed it away from me.

"Just throw whatever it is in the garbage," Arkady said, standing and brushing himself off.

Radya put her hand in the urn. Her fingertips emerged looking as if they had been turned to dust. The ashes sparkled in the light. For a moment I thought I saw my mother's form taking shape in the floating ash, but Arkady's flailing arms disrupted the vision as he grabbed the urn back from Radya.

"Here, let me help you, Mr. C," I said again, trying to take the urn from him.

"Don't touch it, Stalina," Radya screamed. "Arkady, what is it? What is this? Get it off of me."

"Help my wife while I get rid of this," he said, holding the urn over his head.

"Not the urn, Arkady, I just bought it!" Radya screamed again.

"Oh shut up, woman!" he shouted back at her.

Arkady headed for the balcony off the living room. Radya was chasing after him. My mother's ashes were swirling in the chaos. Out on the balcony Arkady overturned the urn and flung the contents to the wind. I watched as my mother's ashes sailed away from the balcony and out toward the ocean. Radya joined Arkady on the balcony and grabbed the urn from him. As they scrambled, I took a longer look at the photograph on the side table. It was of Arkady with Stalin and Ezhov.

"Don't throw it down there—you'll kill someone."

"Didn't you look inside this thing when you bought it, woman?"

"It was dark in the shop. I thought it was empty."

"Where did you get it? Take it back and get another," he said, handing her the urn. "This one was used—by someone's dead grandmother, apparently."

"The man at the flea market told me it was one of a kind," she said.

"The short guy with the crucifix tattooed on his neck. What's his name, Jesus?" he asked.

"Arkady, his name is Rafael, but everyone calls him Shorty. The flea market reminds me of the ones at home," she added.

"They're all con artists, Radya; of course they want you to think there is no other like it," he said as he turned to come back inside.

My mother had clearly exacted her revenge. Any disruption to their perfect little life would have pleased her.

"Thank you both for your hospitality. I really must be going. Is there anything I can do to help?" I asked.

I had taken the photograph from the table and was hiding it behind my back. I wanted it to add to my collection and to remember this day. The Chernovskys might miss it, but I did not care.

"Nadia wanted us to take you to the boardwalk," Radya said.

"That's perfectly fine. I can go myself," I said. "I should be getting back to Connecticut soon."

"Stalina, why did you come to Brooklyn?" Arkady asked.

"My mother sent me to take vengeance for my father's disappearance and ugly demise."

Arkady laughed. "He wore the wrong hat; he could not stay among us."

"Arkady, how could you?" Radya said as she fidgeted with a doily from one of the tables.

Now I knew the truth.

"I'm just kidding, Stalina. No one will ever know why your father was sent away."

"Actually, I came because I heard there were good bookstores on Brighton Avenue with Russian newspapers and books. I was homesick for them."

They both stared at each other silently, and then Arkady got his voice. "The best shop is called St. Petersburg," Arkady said.

"I like the one next to M&I," Radya said.

"M&I, that's where I had the coffee that burned my throat," I said.

"They always keep their coffee too hot," Arkady said.

"But they make the most delicious meringue cake with chocolate and walnuts," Radya added.

"I actually heard someone talking about it on the street," I said.

I had to get away from them. There's something foul about informers, and Radya and Arkady had started to reek. They made me ill. "I'll stop there on my way to the bookstore. I better get going," I added.

"Stalina, I forgot to ask you with all the confusion—how is your mother?"

"Radya, would you let the poor girl go," Arkady said as he grabbed another handful of sunflower seeds.

I looked at the urn. Both of them looked at me looking at the urn.

"Nadia didn't tell you?" I said. "My mother passed away in Petersburg not long ago."

"Where is…" Radya tried to ask.

"I had her cremated."

"And her ashes?" Arkady asked.

"Scattered in the Baltic Sea," I said.

"Radya, maybe this urn you bought was filled with someone's ashes. I feel sick," Arkady said.

"Oh Arkady, stop fussing. Whatever it was is gone. Stalina, your mother will be happy in the sea; she was a beautiful swimmer. I am sorry for your loss," Radya said.

"Thank you, I appreciate your hospitality," I said. I felt my palm sweating as it clutched the photograph. I grabbed my bag and held it behind my back as I slipped the frame into a side pocket.

Arkady's mouth was already filled with sunflower seeds when I went to shake his hand. He nodded and said nothing. The door closed behind me with a whoosh of air from the vacuum created in the windowless corridor.

I spoke to my mother on the way down in the elevator. "Thank you, Mother, for the amusing show. Your ashes went out to sea over the rooftops of Brooklyn. Now you cover half the globe. It's better that we sent you out to sea; otherwise you'd be trapped in that apartment with the Chernovskys.

The urn, your ashes—what a mess you made all over their fancy-schmancy furniture. It was all very amusing."

I could see my mother nodding her head in agreement. Whenever she acknowledged something, she would close her eyes as if to trap it in her soul. My mother liked to hold on to things. Hate, ribbons, Stalin, and her wedding ring. Being a mother was the only thing she could not hold on to. Hers was a cold distance she never learned to control. After the siege, she was simply waiting, for a strong cup of tea, for Stalin's henchmen to take my father, for me to leave, and for death. She was always far away. I pulled the photograph out of my bag and looked at it once more, feeling slightly woozy from the whole encounter, or maybe it was just because the elevator wobbled on its way down to the lobby.

Outside on Neptune Avenue, the wind greeted me like a wall. I leaned into it and walked as if climbing the Altai Mountains. I grabbed my collar and pulled my coat closed. Breathing in the salted, slanted air put a big sting in my lungs that reminded me of home.

St. Petersburg, the name of the bookstore, was scrawled in red neon script above the door like a ribbon of candy. It was a market of videos, magazines, music, and books. A feast from home for an immigrant tourist like myself. There were hundreds of romance and science fiction novels. Pushkin, Tolstoy, and Chekhov were carefully placed for good measure on the narrow, crowded shelves in between the smooth, hard plastic covers. So many, many books. The splashy covers and rough parchment pages were a trip home for my hands and eyes. The Cyrillic letters were like fireworks dancing in front of me. I grabbed a book off the shelf. The cover had an astronaut in the foreground and a blond female alien floating in space behind him. I opened the book to page one and read.

An Astronaut's Dilemma
Chapter One: Asteroid Zero, 2056

Lt. Yuri Griskovksy tied his bootlaces and thought about the general's wife flirting with him at the state dinner the night before. Fanya was her name, and she was a lot younger than her husband. She had beautiful blue eyes and a petite, athletic figure. He wondered if the flirtation was the reason he was chosen for the extremely dangerous mission, Asteroid Zero. He discovered a handkerchief in his left boot infused with her gardenia perfume. He placed it inside the vest pocket of his flight uniform so that he could take it with him into space.

Romance and space travel—how Russian of you, dear author. I'd buy the sequel also, *Alien Children of the Asteroid's Moon.* Procreation in space—this should make for fascinating reading. In the store's video section they had *Krokodil,* our famous puppet cartoon. *Krokodil Takes a Trip by Train.* I'd bring it as a gift to Nadia for letting me have the day off. Good-bye, Brighton Beach. Next time I'd have the meringue with chocolate and walnuts.

Chapter Twenty-three: Returning Home

The subway rumbled back from the end of its line while the sunlight flickered a little through the tracks and Brighton Avenue was pulled away from me. The light flashed along the tops of babushkas' heads. Women becoming blonds in the beauty salons closed their eyes as the train went past and the fading Cyrillic lettering on the walls disappeared. My eyes were pulsing to the speeding landscape as I went back into the beast and held tight, waiting to be put out at Port Authority and Forty-second Street.

Inside the terminal a man was playing a banjo under a poster of the Statue of Liberty. I would have to save my visit to that torch-wielding lady for another time. The strain of the metal strings vibrated off the steel girders and made the air sweeter. My hips swayed with the beat. I was happy.

"That's right, mama, you move those big ol' scrumptious hips. I'll keep playin' for ya," the musician said with a big smile flashing a gold tooth.

He quickened his rhythm. I sashayed over to his money hat and threw in a dollar.

"You dance like an angel, mama! God is going to want you for his own, but right now I'm glad you're here on earth in the blessed Port Authori-tay!"

"Moscow, Kennedy, Port Authori-tay!" I sang back to him as I made my way outside.

"A world traveler, oh my, my, my!" I heard him sing as I went through the doors.

I wanted a taste of the city once more before getting on the bus. The streets were torn up with huge, gaping holes. Men were working down below. I had seen them years before. Their yellow hard hats still bobbed up and down as buses and cars rumbled past. They looked like residents of a new sub-level city, added to accommodate the masses. I thought of Frederica the palm reader and wanted to see her to tell her how accurate her prediction of betrayal had been. I also thought it would be helpful to have her tell me something else about my future. But when I turned the corner, I saw that her storefront was gone. Only a big, gaping hole remained, empty and blackened like a tooth pulled from a giant's lower jaw. The Christ Almighty Church was still standing, but its side wall was now exposed. There was an advertisement on the wall. The faded letters read:

Dancers
All Shapes & Sizes
Men
Come to
"A Cheap Way to Heaven"
Five Cents
for Six Minutes
Right Around
the Corner

The words were transparent like clouds disappearing into a mountainside. A church wall advertising a peep show? I would expect that in Russia, but here in New York, it was a welcome sight for me. It was almost like a poem, and it made me feel even more at home. A Cheap Way to Heaven was still there, but the sign above their door said "Fifty Cents a Minute." I wondered what would happen if I raised the rates at the Liberty. The cost of linens had recently gone up.

On a fence where Frederica's storefront had been, a sign read, "Site of Bank of America's Midtown Branch." Frederica's crystal ball was nowhere to be seen.What a shame, this city changed almost as fast as the ruble.

The Liberty Motel in Berlin, Connecticut, was now my home. I'd be going home now. With my mother's revenge complete, I was free to go. I'd be glad to leave this city. It was so dirty. No one here bent over to pick up their trash. The garbage stayed where it was dropped and became part of the scenery. Amalia's son, Alexi, told me why this was so.

"It's very American," he explained one morning in the kitchen when I asked him why people threw their garbage out car windows.

Alexi at sixteen had embraced the American luxuries of boredom, disdain for adults, a passion for privacy, and everything disposable. But he would still do anything his mother asked, even steal, and with that he remained Russian.

"It's someone's job. They get paid to pick up after us," he added, leaving for school with his shirttails hanging out.

* * *

The buses waiting to depart from the bowels of Port Authority were like fidgeting horses with their rears swaying in impatience to be fed. The front seat with the picture window next to the driver afforded the best view, and as I was first in line, this place of privilege was mine. The bus left the city out the back end of Port Authority. These backstreets were dark and deserted even with the last pieces of sunlight holding onto the sky between the buildings. The few people we passed on the street looked up at the bus as if they yearned to leave the city, too. The alleys felt like places where secrets are kept.

Stopped at a light before we entered the tunnel, my question about Frederica's whereabouts was answered. A folding table with a crystal ball was set up in front of a building, and there she sat in the same white plastic chair, looking at the split ends in her freshly dyed blond hair. She was taking advantage of a little bit of sunlight bouncing off a window across the street in the brief moment that it was touching her. The bus pushed forward a few inches, cutting off Frederica's light like a prison door slamming shut. She looked up at the bus, the thief of her light. In my bag I found the picture of my parents I had showed her more than two years ago and held it up to the window. Her eyes squinted to see me and the photograph. As the bus pulled away, recognition came to her face. She pointed to her eye as if she wanted me to see something. Then she pointed behind her back. I turned around, and in the seat directly behind me was an old woman, near in age to my mother, wearing a lemon yellow sweater and a lime green beret with a rhinestone pin that said "I Heart NY." I looked back out at the nodding Frederica and then to the old woman whose big, broad smile was exaggerated by pink lipstick applied thickly and sloppily over the edges of her lips. Everything around her, even the deserted streets, suddenly felt carefree and filled with possibility. Frederica flashed me a crooked purple smile, and just as the bus entered the tunnel, she disappeared. The old woman yawned loudly, and I sat back and thanked New York for offering me such hope and humor.

As the bus moved in a northwesterly direction, an intoxicating vista unfolded. Blurring signposts, rail guards, and trees along the highway flashed by as the white lines disappeared underneath the bus and the burning sunset on the driver's horizon gave way to an idea for a new room design. My eyes went dream hazy and I envisioned the "Highway to Heaven Room," or room number three. This new room would take my customers' fantasies to a spectacular place. A vibrating "mobile-a-bed" would transport them with top-down convertible style into a perpetually changing and mesmerizing sunset. The wheels of the car would be textured with fleece and the interior lined with satin. It would have a fur-covered steering wheel, and the back seat would be wide enough for a picnic. There would be vanity mirrors everywhere, and the radio would play whatever station you chose. Regulation seat belts, of course. The sunset machine, a multicolored rotating light, would be timed for the length of your stay. I have always found bus rides in America inspiring.

Epilogue: My Other Blunt Self-Portraits

I like to relax in what was Mr. Suri's favorite heart-shaped tub after a day of serving the needs of my customers. The Liberty Motel can be a wonderful, playful, euphoric place, but it also can be a place of fierce battles and casualties. In any case, every day is a long day, and I look forward to a relaxing, steamy bubble bath. Today while cleaning out the front desk I found a note I never sent to the parents of one of our casualties in the war of love.

This was a few years ago. A pair of teenage lovers went the way of Romeo and Juliet. They left a note that said, "We love this room and each other very much. Good-bye." I sent this note through the police to the families. I hope they are glad to have something from their loved ones and to know that even in such tragedy the motel had given them a place of peace, however briefly.

Bill Clinton had just been elected president, for the second time. It was late on election night and most of the votes were already counted. Carmela and I were not yet citizens, but we watched on the television and ate lots of popcorn, throwing bits to the cats. In Russia, the elections were never cause for celebration. Democracy was a shadowy illusion of the Kremlin. Elections were always landslides. Little did we know that while we amused ourselves, and Bill Clinton was

185

basking in his triumphant second win, the desperate couple was drinking a poisonous cocktail.

I made my usual fifteen-minute warning call to the room, the Caribbean Sunset Room. After several calls with no response, I went in and found the young lovers in each other's arms, dead. The double suicide made the tabloid papers. Apparently the young fellow had spurned the older sister of his beloved. The rejected sister went mad and had to be institutionalized. The family never forgave him and tried to keep the lovers apart. The papers made him out to be a ruthless cad. I remember seeing them before they went to the room. They seemed simply young and in love. Business slowed down for a while after that, but not for long. This sad story was soon forgotten.

A couple of years after the suicides, there was a death by hanging, but that one never made the papers. President Clinton was in the news again. This time it was about a stain on a stocky girl's dress. I never understood what the problem was. I can understand his wife being upset, but he's a man—they are known for losing their minds when it comes to what my mother used to affectionately call their "Monsieur Mindless."

* * *

"Tell your lover, 'I miss your Monsieur Mindless,'" my mother said to me one night. "It never fails to fluster them, but men like to know you are thinking about them. Miss your, *monsieur*—get it, Stalina?" She was simply being philosophical about men. Her experience was limited to my father and Maxim, but her delusions made her expansive with advice. She knew English and French and would mix the languages in our conversations often. I was very confused, and had been crying about Trofim.

"Yes, Mother, I miss his Monsieur Mindless," I said.

"Don't bother with him; he's a two-faced snob. You can always find someone else to fuck."

I was too shocked to react, beyond choking back my tears. When I told my friends the expression, they thought my mother was hysterically funny. I informed them that she was losing her mind. My friends still loved the expression, and when we would gossip about the men in or out of our lives, "Monsieur Mindless" was always there. Sometimes I still miss Trofim, but luckily, I live here at the motel and have this red heart-shaped tub to soak away any troubles in the water and bubbles.

* * *

That terrible night, a fellow who had been to the motel several times, always with a different woman, rented the "Roller Coaster Fun Park" for two hours. After half an hour he came to the front desk to get change for a fifty-dollar bill. I got a better look at him and saw how strangely he was dressed. His black raincoat had a fur collar, and his head was covered with a baseball cap that had "I Love Berlin" embroidered in red across the front. Previously, I remembered him being bald, but this time he had chin-length black hair sticking out from under the hat. I recognized him for the distinctive pockmarks on his face that had the shape of half moons on both his high cheekbones. He usually signed in as Santa Claus, but that day he signed the name Julius Caesar.

"Hello, how are you today?" I gave him my usual greeting.

"You recognize me?" he shot back.

"It's your handwriting. Santa Caesar, Julius Claus, it makes no difference—you have a very distinctive half-moon shape to your…letter *C*, sir."

"Santa Caesar, I like that," he said.

I heard the door to the Roller Coaster Room open, and then a woman's voice. "Hey, what are you doing? I thought you'd be right back. I'm feeling lonely all by myself in here." She had left the door half open.

To my regular customer I said, "Julius Caesar was a very complicated man."

"Was he now? You are a smart little lady."

As he turned to go to the room, he looked back at me and said, "What is now amiss that Caesar and his senate should redress?"

It took me a moment, but I added, "Act Three, Scene Four."

"Act Three, Scene One," he said as he tipped his baseball hat with the wig attached.

He was in the room for less than an hour, and then he left without the woman. As he passed the front desk, he said, "She's resting up for the time we have left. Here's an extra twenty in case she needs more time."

An hour passed, and I heard nothing from the room, and there was no answer to my phone call. A hardening knot of unease began to grow sharp tentacles in my stomach. I chewed an antacid, which helped, but I still felt that something was terribly wrong.

The crow was making a huge racket outside the room. There is an ugly side to the short-stay world, and this was one I would like to say never happened. As I opened the door, the strong smell of the woman's perfume hit me, and then I saw her, a scarf pulled tight around her twisted neck. She was hanging dead from the roller-bed-coaster.

I called the police. Two came quickly. Many of them are my customers. They help to keep my business going smoothly and don't want any trouble for their comrades. The woman, a local prostitute, was one they knew well.

As one of the officers picked his teeth with a matchbook, he said, "We'll call this a suicide. No worries—we'll take care of the body. You can go back to work."

The other officer said, "No need to mention this to anyone, Ms. Folskaya. We've got your back."

"My lips are sealed," I replied. The poor woman; what brought her to such a sad end I can never know.

Most of my work here at the motel is very routine, but as you can see, at times it can try my patience. And as with the events of that night, they can sometimes do much worse. Booking rooms, taking inquiries from hushed voices in random phone booths, or dealing with the demands of my regular customers who act like this is their own private club. This is my life, my work, my world now.

* * *

"What do you mean the Roller Coaster Room is booked?" one of them snapped just the other day.

"Sorry, it's first come first served; that's our policy," I responded.

"But I use the Roller Coaster Room every Thursday at three o'clock. I have now for a year."

"Why not try the Caribbean Room? It's very popular."

He is an older gentleman who always signs himself in as Mark Twain, a local hero here in the Hartford area.

"You've got me over a barrel. She's not going to like it; she likes to eat cotton candy while we…"

"Yes, I understand, but the Caribbean Room has its own romantic charms."

"Maybe I'll bring her a piña colada instead of the cotton candy."

"That's the spirit," I said.

* * *

Time somehow always moves on. Last week Carmela found half a green rubber sexual pleasure device. I believe it is called a *dildo*. It was cut in half and left on the back seat in the Highway to Heaven Room. She never found the other half. People get crazy. I gave her a twenty-dollar bonus for dealing with that, and we had a good laugh. Another time a pair of fur-covered handcuffs was left in the Gazebo Room locked onto one of the bedposts. We had to dismantle the bed to remove them. Carmela wanted to give them to her boyfriend, but I warned her that without the key they could prove to be dangerous. She hung them on the wall of the linen room, where the cats love to swat at them. Yes, now we have more than one cat. Amalia recently went back to Russia to take care of her mother and left her cats, Shosta and Kovich, at the motel with me.

"They always liked you better," she said when she brought them by the motel before leaving.

I would miss my old friend. It was hard to hold a grudge after so long, and her referrals from the Majik Cleaning Agency were always very helpful at the motel. We talked about the bras and everything else.

"The past is the past," I told her. "Both the good and the bad."

"I am sorry, Stalina, it was a time when I had much confusion. And little money."

"You are a survivor, Amalia; we both are. I have many reasons to be grateful to you. Go to your mother; she needs you. I can promise you your cats will have a good life here at my motel."

Shosta and Kovich are that special breed of cat born and bred in Leningrad. Not many cats survived the siege, but the ones that did produced a very hardy strain of felines. These tough cats are a big part of the city's post-Soviet economy. The babushkas rescue the kittens from back alleys, sewers, and roofs and then sell them on bridges and corners near metro stations. Shosta and Kovich have become fat and lazy here in America, but occasionally they show their "Leningrad" side. They hunt with Svetlana, who learned everything from her surrogate mother, Zarzamora. The only photograph I took of Svetlana and the crow sits along here with the rest of my photo collection. I believe Shosta and Kovich were jealous of ZZ and her relationship with Svetlana. One day the cats chased the crow across the driveway, and she was struck and killed by a car leaving the motel. Svetlana was shaken, as was I. She did not eat for days and just sat under the pine trees where we buried the poor crow.

All in all, this place is not for the faint of heart. Overdoses and fires. Panty hose stretched, ripped, and tied around pillowcases, cigarettes burning on the edge of the toilet. Once a set of false teeth were found in the cup by the bathroom sink. How could someone forget those? It can all make for a very long day. As I recline in the heart-shaped tub, the photographs are my confidants, and with a glass or two of chilled vodka, my words flow freely. *Nostrovya!*

Thip!

Today, dear friends, marks my tenth anniversary here at the Liberty Motel in 2001. I am now *Citizen* Stalina, no longer *Comrade* Stalina. Giving up on my country was like severing ties with a lover. Like a haunting, sometimes I still catch a smell or see a shadow from a streetlamp that could only be Russia. Carmela and I call each other "comrade." It keeps our spirits up.

To my friends and family pictured before me, I say, "I offer you these blunt portraits to shed light on how the last ten years have been. Please pardon me this indulgence, as I drink in honor of this anniversary and my recent citizenship. *Apeeteeta!*"

Thiip!

Mmm, cold, thick vodka, like a fresh pillow against my face.

A toast to Nadia, my ex-boss and autocratic friend, who left five years ago to take her parents back to Petersburg to die. Without her I would not have the Liberty Motel. The other motels she put in the hands of her black suit boys. I am proud to say that our short-stay empire is thriving along Windsor Avenue here in Berlin, Connecticut. The city is still dying, and lucky for us, because as the city continues in a spiral down its sinkhole of recession, our short-stay motels continue to flourish.

To short stays and long sips! *Spaseeba! Nadia!*
Thiip!

I made Carmela my business partner. She knows beauty well and has used her love of the land when decorating our special rooms. She was inspired to complete the Caribbean Room, and she was thoughtful enough to incorporate my idea for the "cabana-bed" into the design, which pleased me very much. My most loyal customers, Joanie and Harry, waited with great anticipation for the completion of that room. Ten years after the "roller coaster" incident, they are still conducting their affair "on the side," as they put it. Neither one wants to give up the other, so they accept their situation with dignity and are pleased to have a place like the Liberty to come to.

A toast to inspired romantic settings and Strauss and Sons Hardware, the local store where we buy everything to decorate the rooms! They always have everything I need, no matter how big or small.

Thiip!

The vodka when chilled correctly is so very smooth.

Carmela molded the blue carpet in the Caribbean Sunset Room into a theater of waves surrounding the cabana-bed, which stands on stilts and has a thatched roof. When the door opens, sounds of the ocean begin to play over and over. She is very, very clever. Harry likes the wraparound sunset mural painted on three walls.

"You see it from all sides when you are lying in the cabana-bed," Harry says. "It's all very intoxicating."

Joanie told me soon after the room was finished, "Harry got me some fancy-schmancy jasmine perfume for our 'Caribbean' time. Maybe someday we'll go to the real Caribbean. Until then, your rooms will have to do, Stalina."

That was six years ago. They have yet to visit the "real" Caribbean.

"Ginger and coconut are other scents you might want to try. I hear they can be very enticing," I told her one day when she was returning the key.

After she tried the new scents, she reported back to me. "The coconut made Harry sneeze, and the ginger made him itch where his thumb is missing."

That's when Joanie told me the story of how Harry lost his thumb.

"Harry used to run away when he was a boy from his home in Brooklyn. His father fought in World War II, was very strict, and wanted to punish him after he found him hitchhiking onto the BQE for the fifth time. Can you imagine? It's amazing Harry survived; he was only twelve years old. His father set the dog after him. The dog grabbed his hand, and as Harry tried to slip away, the dog's jaw locked down on his thumb. Harry's mother ran away with him from the hospital in the middle of the night. She left Brooklyn and moved here to Berlin and got a job in an umbrella factory. They heard later his father put his head in the oven in their apartment in Canarsie. The neighbors smelled gas and called the police. His father was still alive but unconscious. They revived him, but he was like a three-year-old. When his mother died, Harry went to the nursing home where his father lived. He took a gun and a bottle of arsenic, but he could not kill him. The drooling, rocking, and loud cartoons got to Harry. He told me the story when we were in high school. That's when I fell in love with him. He's a real mensch."

A toast to your love, Harry and Joanie, my most loyal customers.

Thiiip!

Mmm, peppery, this vodka is.

Nadia wrote after her parents passed away within a month of each other.

Dear Stalina,

My parents are gone. Putin gave them special honors. They were mentors to young "Vladi" in his early KGB days. Did you know it is illegal to spread human ashes in Russia? I had no idea. I put their remains together in a Chinese urn my mother kept on her mantel in Brooklyn. You may have seen it when you visited them. She brought it with her when they left Brighton Beach. They sold many of their things at a flea market at the beach before they left. I wish they had kept some of their photographs from Russia. My father had a photo taken with Stalin. You can get good money for that sort of Soviet memorabilia. But the urn my mother refused to sell. It was a very valuable antique that my father purchased on one of his trips to China. I keep it by my bedside. I miss them very much. Petersburg is more beautiful than ever. Much is happening here for the three-hundred-year celebration, and of course the mafia still runs the city, so everything functions very well. Why don't you come visit for the festivities?

Your friend and comrade,
Nadia

Oh dear urn, you earned your keep. What liars Nadia's parents were! Maxim never mentioned anything about it being illegal when he spread my mother's ashes in the Baltic Sea.

Thiip!

Mmm, the vodka is just the right viscosity.

Among the photographs surrounding me is the one I took from Arkady and Radya's glass side table in Brighton

Beach. It was from a photo booth arcade with a fake setup where you could have your picture taken with our leaders, Stalin and Ezhov standing next to a bridge in Leningrad. Trofim had the same photograph, but in his, which was taken later than Arkady's, Ezhov had been airbrushed away. It was for this version I scolded my lover.

He would argue, "It's for protection, Stalina, just like your name. I got a deal at the photo booth. They gave me extra copies. Would you like one?"

"You do look handsome on that bridge."

I did take one of the copies, but the photograph was not enough to protect my dear Trofim. His students thought he went mad when one of them saw him eating a slice of Lysenko's brain on a piece of sourdough bread and reported him to the authorities. The police did not mind his charade with the calf brain; they actually knew about it because the KGB had Lysenko's real brain. It was Trofim's experiments to improve Mendeleev's vodka recipe that ended up being the final straw. The KGB did not want anyone changing what they already considered flawless. Olga sent me the article from *Pravda*, which I have taped to the back of the photograph.

Thiip!

It reads,

St. Petersburg
April 15, 2002
Physicist Found Dead in Vat of Chilled Vodka

The body of physicist Trofim Nayakovsky, who had been missing for several years, was found dead in his former lab at St. Petersburg University. He was thought to have gone crazy after a student saw him consuming a slice of a hu-

man brain, and soon after he disappeared with no trace. His body, preserved in a vat of chilled vodka, was found when renovations for the tercentennial started and the lab's refrigerated vault was emptied. Death by drowning was determined, as it was hard to tell at so late a date if there were any signs of a struggle. One of his former students said that after he was seen eating what was thought to be a piece of our scientist Lysenko's brain, the authorities started making inquiries about the professor's activities. The student, who wishes to remain anonymous, told the authorities that in addition, the professor's teaching had become scattered and erratic, and he was obsessed with developing a new recipe for vodka. The brain was actually that of a calf. The vat filled with vodka, in which Prof. Nayakovsky was discovered, had been placed inside a large centrifuge that was being stored inside the cold vault. Relatives were contacted, and after the body thawed, they requested cremation. He is survived by his wife, Tatiana, and children Yosip and Nina. During the next year, many institutions are having facelifts in preparation for the upcoming celebrations. We wonder what other surprising discoveries will be made.

Liars! Trofim would not have been so stupid as to fall into the vat and let the lid close. If he was that well preserved, instead of cremation, maybe they should have put him on display at the Academy of Science next to the jar with the African Pygmy.

Olga wrote a note below the article. "Bollocks! Stalina, can you believe how they covered up this one? Poor Trofim, at least he was drunk when he went."

Nostrovya! To you Olga, my dear friend and legendary hairdresser!

Thiip!

At least I can look forward to the possibility of Trofim greeting me when it's my time to go. A toast to my dear love, Trofim! My heart still aches for you, Trofim.

Thiip!

Mr. Suri sent me pictures of his laundromat in Tucson, Arizona. He wrote on the back, "Stalina, we have named our business 'Liberty Laundry' in honor of the motel, our favorite tourist site, and it also reminds me of you."

Prost! A toast to you, Mr. Suri, and your heart-shaped tub which I have filled with bubbles of a lavender scent for its therapeutic qualities of relaxation and contemplation. I think of you often.

Thiip!

Still I have not made it for a visit to the real Lady Liberty. She has been closed to the public for the time being. The brochures I have read say that it is a thrilling view from statue's crown. There have been some hard times on these shores, and many restrictions have been enforced. What a shame, and it is all just after I became a citizen.

Nostrovya! Lady Liberty! To the day when you are free again to have visitors touch your robes and appreciate your toes.

Thiip!

They say she is very shapely underneath all the drapery. Her measurements are thirty-six, thirty-five, thirty-six—feet, of course. She's a voluptuous, big-boned gal, very Russian. An immigrant just like myself. From France she hails, not Russia, but the French always loved the Russians and vice versa, so I can imagine that Mr. Sculptor Bartholdi had one or two Russian models to base his lady on. The officials say it was his mother he used, but I tend to think with such a figure underneath her skirts, it was one of his many lovers. Like many artists, he had a reputation for being a ladies' man.

I raise an arm to Lady Liberty and her shapely figure. You would look wonderful, dear lady, in one of my imported Russian bras. I'm sure I would have had one to fit your shapely size had they not all been stolen from me.

Thiip!

I heard from Amalia. That thief! It's sad we are no longer friends; there's so much between us—good and bad—that can never go away. Her mother passed away. I knew how difficult it would be, so I did what I could to help her understand what was coming. She thanked me for the push to go home so she could say a proper good-bye. The Magik Cleaning Agency has folded without her special business sense, and she has become very successful in Petersburg. She was one of the first to start a business to introduce American men to Russian women. Now the classifieds in the *St. Petersburg Times* are filled with ads for such enterprises.

Amalia calls her business Veeshni Kazenoor, or Cherries Casino. The office is upstairs on Nevsky near the Kazan Cathedral. It's just her and a computer and a waiting room with red satin walls. Olga sent me this entry from the computer log written by one of her "lonely" women.

Something is missing in my life, and I know if I could only meet the right man I would be fulfilled, complete. I am divorced and have a young son. I am a doctor and know that I could be caring and healing to you as well. Please choose me as I know

I will satisfy your needs and be a proper and faithful wife. My English is close to perfect. I would like to learn more from you. Choose me please. I wait holding my breath to hear from you.

Ina D.

* * *

Knock! Knock!

"Yes?"

"Stalina, it's Carmela. Shosta and Kovich want to come in and sit by your bath."

The bubbles fascinate those two. I am no longer angry with them for the death of the crow—they are cats, after all—but Svetlana is still the better mouse killer.

"Let them in, Carmela."

I hear two cars leaving the driveway as the door opens, and the cats race in to be the first at tub side.

"Carmela, are things busy tonight?"

The top of Carmela's head and her shiny black hair glisten from the outside light. Her eyes are cast down, even though she knows the tub filled with bubbles conceals all. She has beautiful long eyelashes.

"Yes, three rooms are filled, and two people just finished. You relax. Have you got everything you need?"

"Thank you, I have what I need. The door sticks a bit at the top left corner. I must trim the edges before too long."

"I'll help you with that tomorrow."

"Come sit, Comrade Carmela. Have a bit of vodka with me. I am celebrating."

"Since you are now a U.S. citizen, must I call you Citizen, or do you still prefer Comrade, Stalina?"

"Why not Citizen Comrade? I am celebrating my ten years here at the Liberty Motel!"

"A quick toast, then. I have to go clean the rooms and mind the desk. Remember, we have a business to run."

"You are a feisty one, Carmela. Come sit for a moment; we'll hear when someone comes up the drive. Take another cup from the bathroom. Close the door."

Shosta and Kovich are circling the tub, sniffing the lavender bubbles that have escaped over the sides.

"*Cht, cht, cht.* Come here, comrade kitties, I'll blow some bubbles for you."

The bubbles scooped in my hands are soft as silk. They tickle my palm the way Trofim used to when we would sit at our favorite tea shop near the Moika Bridge. He'd make a circle with his finger in my hand and then move it up to my lips to test which was softer, the lips or the palm. When my lips were dry, he would kiss them. When my palm was dry, he would massage my hand until it sweated just a bit. The lavender bubbles do just the same. Shosta and Kovich know the game; they wait for me to blow the bubbles in their direction.

"Here's some bubbles...*ffft!* For you, Shosta! *Ffft!* For you, Kovich! Come, Carmela, pull up a chair."

"Stalina, how many toasts have you made tonight?"

"Bubbles floating on the air like my head from the vodka."

"I'll join you."

"To each of these rogues in my gallery of photographs, and now to you, the best partner a bubble-soaked Russian could ever have! *Nostrovya!*"

Thiip! Thiip!

"Shosta and Kovich don't care which country you call your own, as long as they have their bubbles," Carmela said.

"To Shosta and Kovich, the expatriated cats, and their undying devotion to eating, sleeping, and bubble play. If only they would speak, so we could truly converse. It's the same problem Alice had," I responded expansively.

"I am sorry, Stalina, I don't know any Alice."

"Yes you do, from the book."

"The one about the mirror?"

"The looking glass, yes. Alice thought if a purr meant yes and a mew meant no, then at least we could have a conversation with them."

"I always thought a purr meant 'I am content,' and a mew meant 'I need.'"

"That's the spirit, Carmela."

Thiip! Thiip!

"You have taught me how to enjoy your country's drink, Stalina."

As Carmela tipped her head back to take down the vodka, I noticed a jagged scar behind her right ear that I had never seen before.

"Carmela, what do you dream of?" I asked her.

She thought for a moment as she pulled her hair back behind her ear and covered the scar. She seemed self-conscious that I had seen it.

She said, "Juan Mendoza, I dream about him often. I left him at the bar of the Hotel Nacional in Managua. His letters stopped coming soon after I arrived here."

"Sandinista?"

"Schoolteacher."

"Dangerous."

"Apparently to someone."

"Alive?"

"I do not know. From what I could tell, it was safer for both of us not to have contact."

"You will hear about him one day."

"Oww! Shosta, you little…" Carmela cried out.

Shosta, the cat with the single white stripe down its face, had been watching the empty plastic cup that Carmela was spinning on her finger as she told me about Juan Mendoza. The cat could not help herself and jumped on her lap, batted the cup, and scratched her wrist in the process. The disruption brought me a shock of sobriety. My head spun as I sat up.

"Wash your hand, Carmela."

"I have some alcohol in the office."

"We have alcohol right here. Mendeleev's original."

"You finish your bath, Stalina. I need to go back to the desk anyway. It's only a scratch."

The two cats sit side by side cleaning their paws, oblivious to the disruption. "Leave the cats here, Carmela. I'll take them back to the linen room when I finish."

"Very well, Stalina."

As she opens the door, the cats turn to see the outside. The wind has picked up, and on the gust that came through the door, the comforting smell of pine trees—like in Russia—comes into the room. Carmela closes the door with some trouble against the wind. Damn sticking door, the whole room shakes when it closes.

Under the water I slip. Submerged, face up, eyes open. The bubbles have spread. The surface looks solid like ice the color of a stream in winter. A soft blue green. I can hold my breath under water for a long time. I learned from my mother, who had great lung capacity from years of water ballet team. Looking up through the water and bubbles it's like seeing Petersburg through a window on a snowy day. In winter when it snowed the city would be a bit warmer, and steam would rise from the streets. The city with its frozen waterways welcomed the floating, drifting snow. The steam off the street was breaths between hardened pedestrians ducking into metro stops, tea stalls, and museums for relief. On days like these I would wander to my favorite place in Petersburg, the Museum of the Arctic. In the former Church of St. Nicholas, right around the corner from Dostoyevsky's house. St. Nicholas! Santa Claus! In the Arctic! Oh, Russians are clever. As you enter the museum, suspended overhead is the plane that Soviet pilot and hero Valery Chkalov flew from Moscow to America via the North Pole. Standing below the plane was like being a scientist at a remote site waiting for the arrival of monthly supplies. Sometimes here at the Liberty I feel like a fact-finder dumped in a faraway land, researching the human condition as it relates to the need for companionship. My research has become these "Rooms for the Imaginative." Someday I will make a scientific study based on the popularity and longevity of the short-stay phenomenon. Why not? Once a scientist always a scientist.

The Museum of the Arctic has in its collection the head of a woolly mammoth. The first time I touched his ancient, hairy brow, I felt pity for him and his earthly demise. Lost in the cold, frozen to death, despite his long, warm coat. After paying my respects to the mammoth, I would go upstairs to visit the sculptures of indigenous peoples. These people were the ones, it seems, who invented the original "dildo." Not from green rubber, but out of bone and walrus tusks, they made some goodly sized facsimiles. I wonder how the school groups discuss the relevance of such objects in the native cultures. I could start my own museum at the Liberty Motel.

I was often the only person visiting the museum on these days. The quiet and solitude gave me time to imagine the faraway places I wanted to know and a life outside of Russia. Not something I talked to many people about. As I would make my way upstairs, the museum minder—an old woman who recognized me from my frequent visits and knew I loved the museum almost as much as she did—would turn off the lights on the other floors to conserve the electricity. With the lights still off, she would guide me back downstairs with a flashlight and bring me to a favorite diorama. The old lady would flick the switch below a glass display window. Slowly the lights would start to shimmer and glow, and the miniature scene of a lone Arctic research station and its single bare bulb in the window burning in the long winter night would be just a shadow under the moving colors and iridescent shimmering haze. I would stand and stare, and the old woman would watch with me and laugh a little as she whispered, "Aurora borealis, aurora borealis." And I would say, "*Da, prevyet,* aurora borealis." After a minute or so, I would close my eyes and make everything go to black. The silence of the museum would surround me, and I would feel like I was suspended in a warm cloud, much the same as I am here in the heart-shaped tub with the faint smell of lavender surrounding me. She, the museum minder, wore lavender perfume.

Whhoosh, hahhh!

Out from under the water, my breath restored, memory intact and fingers wrinkled like the mammoth's brow. The Liberty Motel is my museum! My rooms are a singular collection, the history of fantasies of pleasure, all preserved and frozen in time. The guests bring life to the exhibits, and I am honored to be the minder.

To my dear family and friends, who will inhabit me forever, I bring you along with me, for it is you that keep the swing in my ever-shifting hips and inspire me to provide a place for happiness, recovery, and when needed, a dose of revenge.

Thiip!

I'll finish up here and count the dollars we brought in and look to see who signed the register tonight. Mark Twain, Alfred Smith, Leo Tolstoy, Harry and Joanie to be sure.

Thiip!

Good night.

THE END

About the Author

Photo by Billy Tompkins

Emily Rubin's fiction has been published in the *Red Rock Review, Confrontations,* and *HAPPY,* and she is a past nominee for the Pushcart Prize. In 2005, she began producing *Dirty Laundry: Loads of Prose,* a reading series that takes place in laundromats around the United States. She divides her time between New York City and Columbia County, New York, with her husband, Leslie, and their dog, Sebastian.